MY BROTHER'S KEEPER

BOOK I

A Novel

Billie Dureyea Shell

This book is dedicated to:

William Ewell & Sky Holsey, we need more people to do what this sister did. If we want these BullShit police to do there job we going to have to make them, black lives matter but we have to make sure that they also matter to us. If you see a police pull one of your folks over take the time to pull over and get involved the time that you take to let them know that you care about what's going on with your brother's and sisters and that you are your brother's keeper an got there back Just might be what saves their lives. So let's make them respect this black lives matter movement but first it starts by us loving each other and respecting ourselves....... My niggas the revolution will not be televised that doesn't mean we can't keep our own records of what happened let's make this shit count..........

Author

Billie Dureyea Shell

Team Shell

Author's Notes

This My Way Of Showing All by My Niggas From My City Love Once one Of Us Get Up We Need To Help The Next Do The Same Real Spit.... This My Boy Jyvontaye Harris AKA Fat Boy From Watts My Nogga Do his Shit Wit This Poerty His Book Will Be coming Soon If y'all like His Shit say So In The Reviews You Leave For The Book I'ma Let Y'all Gone And Turn The Page So You Can Read be My Lil Bra Poem........

AND ENJOY MY BROTHERS KEEPER BOOK 1

Billie Dureyea Shell
Author

MY BROTHER'S KEEP
A poem
By Jyvontaye Harris

Lost in the struggle, mentally unstable but everyone not able to call each other brothers. It wasn't easy going up in the city of Compton and Watts you must learn to stay dangerous meaning kill or be killed remember there's no exceptions when you talk to them cops. I try to keep my head above water, it's hard when the blue shirts breathing down your neck. Police brutality was common in my area when encounter was met with disrespect. Every day I pray for better days seeing too many die at an early age. Prayers go out to the ones that are in a cage. Life sentences is given to the underage. Survival is always a must if you trying to make it to another phase, it's crazy how in order to get peace you got to go to war before you get it. Every day it feels like I'm on the front line, protecting minds and at the same time trying to mind my own business. I will always watch my brother's back the weapon I carry is for my own safety one slip up will have a lot of people who love me emotions mixed up. Everyday my loved ones pray that I make it home safely, and even though I act like I'm too hard to do it I also pray that I make it home to my wife and my baby. Trying to mask the pain I feel inside but it's too hard when it's obvious every wound these streets then gave me the left deep scars yes I'm My Brother's Keeper I don't have a choice I have to be but while I'm watching my brother's back who the fuck is watching me

ACKNOWLEDGEMENT

First and foremost I have to give honor to My Lord And Saviour Jesus Christ without him now of this would be possible. 2020 was a MUTHA FUCCA Corona Virus made shit hard 4 niggas but we made it threw y'all keep your head up and know that God got us, no matter they throw in our way no one can stop what God has plan for you...
Its 2021 now FUCC 2020 and Covid 19.... Now to my family momma I love you and you no I got you no matter what. You mean the world 2 me oh and NO MORE PINCHING LOL.
To my little sister Glenda I love you blackie, you No I Got You always

To my Wife Shatoya Shell you get on my damn nerves ⬢ but I wouldnt trade you 4 anything In the world I love ♥ you more then words can ever express. To all my children 🙏 I love y'all Jazmine, Ant'Tuan, Davon, Anthony, David, Lil Dureyea, Alura, Queen Diavion, Cameron, Preniece, Shaniece and Tajh I love u all and I'll 4ever have ur back you all give me a reason 2 smile... to my cousin Zane RIP nigga I miss u more then anyone will ever no, your always remembered love you bro. to my cousin Ty I miss you thank 4 looking out 4 me and Zane you played a big part in my life and I always looked up to you I love you... Uncle Woody I miss you and love you, you no your my favorite uncle... To my nigga Jamal love you, my brothers Lawrence and fred thank 4 showing me the game I love yall 4 that. To my oldest sister Nedra love you thank you 4 always having my back. to my family uncles anties cousins etc.. I love y'all even those of you that act funny as fuck

To my dark side niggas y'all no what it is YAAH GANG....
Now to all my readers and fans I love you thanks for reading I
hope u enjoy this book as much as I enjoy writing
them with this Corona Virus 19 shit there ain't shit to do but
write so I'm on my shit with that being said y'all be safe cover
your face and love each other life is short so love the ones that
really love I'm gone no. enjoy the book

STAY SAFE

Author Billie Dureyea Shell

THERE'S NOTHING U CANNOT DO

IF U PUT UR MIND 2 IT.

All you nigga's got EDD money so aint no excuse

why you can't get a book LOL

Prologue
JAR SIMMONS

Jar Simmons sat in his office, reviewing some last-minute paperwork. He was in a hurry but had to finish. It's how his family eats. Tonight, he was taking his beautiful wife Noti out on a date for their 20th anniversary. He planned a romantic cruise around town in their limousine. They would go dancing and spend the night together in an exclusive penthouse. Twenty years of marriage and she still holds the key to his heart. He bought her a new 15 carat, emerald cut diamond ring worth one million dollars. The piece was astonishing. He was ready to run out of his shoes to give it to her. Life was good. Jar remembered taking his wife shopping for a new watch on her birthday. It became an afterthought in just five minutes, something else that held her absolute attention. It was a beautiful diamond ring. He stood back, taking in his woman marveling over it. She was captivated. He had to admit the ring was gorgeous. The very next day, he purchased the ring without her knowledge. For two long, hard fought weeks, he kept the ring a secret. She had a way of finding out when he kept something from her. This time, he tried not to look or act any differently. The ring was safe and he wouldn't fall under her spell. A simple touch from her could provoke any man. She was dangerously beautiful. He finally finished the paperwork. His body felt stiff from sitting in one position for so long. He stretched his arms and legs before he got up from the desk, it took him five steps to get to the file cabinet. He put the papers away and then retrieved his coat from the closet by the front door. He grabbed his car keys off the desk and hurried to the exit. Seconds after leaving the place, his feet froze. He stood there, something inside, telling him to stop. He checked the doorknob to see if it was locked. "C'mon." He muttered to himself. He realized he left the ring on the desk. He patted himself down to double check, nothing, then he unlocked the door. After taking a step in, he heard a familiar voice. "It's over," A harsh voice spoke. Jar felt a brutal blow to the back of his head. His legs buckled and he fell to the ground. Somehow, he gathered the strength to roll over onto his back. He couldn't see a thing, everything in view was blurry. He held the back of his head. The feeling of blood leaking through his fingers didn't feel so good. His eyesight regained focus and he was able to see his assailant. "You," He groaned in agony. "I always knew it would be you." The gunman stood firm over Jar and pressed the gun to his face. "I guess you were correct about something for the first time in your despicable life." He smirked. "Please," Jar pleaded for his life. "Don't do this-" He was interrupted. The gunman fired two shots in Jar's face. Large chunks of his head erupted like tiny volcanos filled with blood. The gun exploded a second time. His entire body jerked as if each bullet was a volt of electricity. Three large sections of his suit jacket had disintegrated into the air. His chest settled as his breathing stopped. His only regret was seeing the person who killed him.

Chapter 1
1993

"Jar, wake up!" Noti pushed her husband as her pains grew worse. "Please, I need you." She cried out in agony. The pregnancy was moving into the final stage, labor. This is the worst pain she has ever felt in her life. She calendared the entire nine months. She knew from the day they decided to start a family in March, a baby could arrive in December. Today is a special day, Christmas Eve. And there is not a more painful feeling than labor. She cried louder, wanting to get to the hospital. Jar heard his wife crying while he was asleep. He slowly rolled over to face her. "Hey, honey. What's wrong?" He asked sleepily. She gripped his shoulder and squeezed. "What's wrong," She yelled. "Your child is trying to kill me!" He felt like the Incredible Hulk gripped him by the shoulder. The pain showed all over his face. It was hard to respond. "My... child?" She groaned and applied more pressure to his shoulder. "Yes… our baby is on the way, I need to get to a hospital… now." Jar thought he heard his shoulder pop. He was wide awake, thanks to her tiger grip. She's in labor, he thought. "Shit. You're in labor." He noticed sweat across her forehead. This was serious. He rushed out of bed while she remained lock to his shoulder. He caused her to fall over on her side unexpectedly. His mind started to race. He knew what he had to do. They had taken baby classes together. He remembered the step by step guide he had to master about pregnancy procedures, every meeting he had to attend, and all the training videos he watched. It was time to put his new skills to use. He got dressed quickly, putting on whatever he could find. It didn't matter if the clothes matched or if he had worn them the day before. After he was fully dressed, he found his wife something to wear. He helped her up and swiftly got her ready. He struggled to get her out of the room. When they entered the hallway, he called for his maid, Nina. She came running down the hall to aid them. "It's time?" She asked Jar while giving him a helping hand. She placed her arm around Noti to help support her to the front of their mansion. She was always on standby and alert. She was hired precisely for that reason. During Noti's pregnancy, Jar hired Nina to aid his wife with everything she needed when he was away on business. "Yes, she's in labor. We have to hurry." He responded before opening the front door. They stopped at the front driveway. If he had one wish, he would ask to take away her pain. Every sound she made pierced his heart. He cared about her more than anything in life. "Nina, hold her straight up, I'll get the car." "Yes, sir." She replied. She held Noti firmly in her arms. "Thank you." He said before rushing over to open the garage. He unlocked the Aston Martin, the engine roared to life. He drove the beautiful car back to them and opened the passenger door. He assisted Noti inside the vehicle. He strapped on her seatbelt and closed the door. The hard part was over. He thanked Nina for her assistance before getting back into the sports car. He was on the move and without noticing, slid over the hood of the vehicle like Will Smith in an action movie. He got in the car and sped away from the property. The car raced through traffic as he gunned the V-12 to the hospital. Luckily, the police didn't give him any problems. He pushed the motor well over a hundred. They safely arrived at the hospital. He rushed inside to get help. "My wife is pregnant!" He said frantically. "She's in labor. Please, I need help." Two nurses came rushing out with a wheelchair to assist Noti inside of the building. After what felt like an eternity, Jar witnessed his baby boy being born. They both wanted to keep the gender a surprise until the due date. Suddenly, another boy delivered into the world. They didn't expect twins. Jar never felt a fantastic feeling like this one. He is the father of two wonderful boys. He thought with all the love in his heart to name them. "Let's name them Kane and Abel."

Chapter 2
CHRISTMAS

Jar held both of his newborn boys in his arms, Kane was the firstborn. He weighed eight pounds and two ounces. Abel weighed a solid eight pounds. The boys were identical and looked exactly like their father. Although Kane's hair was a lot longer than Abel's, Kane resembled his father the most because they have similar features. He cradled the boys in his arms, Kane on the right and Abel on the left. He brought Kane closer and kissed him on the forehead, Abel seemed angered by it. He started to pout and began to cry. Every time he kissed Kane before him, Abel would get jealous. He smiled at his son and tried to kiss him. Abel's tiny hand smacked him on the lips. He joked by opening his eyes wide in shock, making Abel giggle. This amused his son and it made him smile. Jar allowed Abel to smack him as many times as he wanted just to keep him happy. There was nothing he loved more than his family. Jar waited with the boys in the recovery room. He stood over the boys while they were asleep. He thought about all the wonderful things in life he wanted to do with them when they were older. He watched two nurses push Noti's bed into the room. He walked over to the door and held it as they guided her inside. They aligned her next to the cradle beside her boys. The nurses told them if they need any assistance, use the controller on the side of the bed, just press the red button in the center. It will send a notification to the nurse's station and somebody will be made available to assist them. Jar thanked them before they left the room. He walked over to his amazing wife of two years. She still looked exhausted from labor. He saw her struggling to get comfortable. He helped by propping some fluffy pillows behind her back. She had worked hard through the pregnancy. He would make sure to be there for her every need, keeping his promise as a husband. A week later, they left the hospital. Jar loved taking care of his family and being there when they needed him. He spoiled the boys. He noticed as Kane grew older, he started to look more like him. Kane's hair grew longer and Noti dreaded it, giving him the same hairstyle. Abel always seemed to get something stuck in his hair. On their third birthday, he managed to find a pair of scissors. He chopped off most of his dreads. Noti found him in the bathroom, scissors in his right, hair in his left. Hair was everywhere, mainly the sink and floor,

Abel had large patches of hair missing. It forced her to shave his head. Since that day, Abel never wanted to grow long hair. There was a time when he tried to cut off Kane's dreads. Noti had stopped him just in time and Abel would use his cute baby voice to get out of trouble. His apologies would cause her to cry. He was the bad one and very close to his mother. She saved him from everything, and he used her to his advantage. Kane was never in trouble. He stayed attached to his father's leg and wanted to go everywhere he went. Noti tried to break him out of it, Kane would cry. When Jar left the house without him, he would cry. Kane would leave Noti if Jar walked into another room. Work was no exception. He brought him on a few occasions. Everyone at the office thought he was a great father for bringing his son. Kane grew on all of them. They treated him like a little brother. On their fifth Christmas, everyone at the office bought Kane a present. When he arrived at home, Abel noticed all his brother's extra gifts. He ran to his mother and cried. Jar explained it was a surprise and didn't know anything about the presents. Later that night, when Kane fell asleep, Abel broke every single gift Kane had... including the extras.

Chapter 3
HIGH SCHOOL -KANE-

It's 2009, my sophomore year of high school. I had grown to be 6'1 and 185lbs. I get along with everyone in the building. They all love me. I'm a beast in three different sports. I play varsity basketball, football and I run track. I love playing ball, but I like running track. That's where I met my first and only girlfriend, Kim. She's a little older but like me. She's a senior and runs for the girls' track team. Man, let me tell you. She's put together. As I got older, I started to take an interest in girls. All my friends have girlfriends. I was the only guy without one. To me, Kim is more beautiful than any girl in the entire school. She has the whole package, a nice ass, breast, gorgeous skin, and a beautiful face. Her brown eyes drive me crazy. And her hair is dreaded like mines. At first, I thought she had mistaken me for somebody else or a senior. I tried to explain to her I wasn't, and she told me it didn't matter. The boys and girls team practiced together. That's when she would bother me. I counted on it every time we stretched before and after practice. She would find a way to get next to me and pull my hair. I used to watch her giggle with her little girlfriends when they spoke to each other. They saw me watching and laughed anyway. I thought something was wrong with me. Later, I learned that it was just a girl thing. My father told me you would know when a girl likes you. She'll do funny shit like pull your hair. That's just the way they act sometimes. When I gained the confidence to ask her out, she answered yes before I could finish the question. That was crazy. It's like she read my mind. My best friend, Simon Jones, is on the track team. He's the fastest person I ever met in my life and we're in the same grade. He ran the forty-yard dash in 4.2 seconds. He won the state title two years straight. I finished behind him with a time of 4.3 seconds. He barely beats me when we compete. The coach said we're the fastest two legs that had ever run for the school. I even gave Simon a nickname and everybody calls him by it, Smoke. When he lines up to run, my boy would say, somebody is about to get smoked. That's exactly what would happen. He'll outrun everybody and I would be the only person who could keep up. Smoke and I took all the titles home. The 100, 200, 400, and the 4x4, we won every race we entered. We even went on a double date for Homecoming. My brother Abel avoided stuff like dancing. A few girls told me he was mean.

Hell, I know that already. What the hell else is new? There is one positive thing about him. He's the smartest person at school. He kept a 4.0 grade point average. He told me only knuckleheads play sports. I asked him if I was a knucklehead? He said yes. I'm in fact, the biggest knucklehead in the entire school. I used to wonder how in the hell did he get all the smarts. True, I have all the skills to play any sport I want, but I'm not nearly as smart as that damn bookworm. My brother and I never get along, not even in school. Our friends belong to two different groups. I hang with the cool crowd and his group made up of tech heads. They all are geniuses. We probably spoke two times out of the entire school year. People don't know we're twins. One day, I came home from practice, and he was locked in his room, crying. I heard him from the hallway. I knocked on the door to figure out what was going on and if I could help. He kept yelling for me to go away. I don't know why, but I didn't. He finally came to the door with a sheet of paper. He held it out to me. It had a grade on it, B plus. I asked, why in the hell are you crying over a B plus? He told me how in the hell he was supposed to take over the world with a fucking B plus. Then he slammed the door in my face. The next day the teacher was brutally beaten with a baseball bat. The alarming part about the situation is that it was my baseball bat. My first trip to jail, murder.

Chapter 4

CLASSROOM LOVE

Two officers walked into the classroom. I was in the fourth period, just another day at school in the middle of taking a test and passing a love note to Kim. Two of my best friends were also in the same class. Bear and Redd. I met Michael Redd while playing basketball for the school. He's the point guard and I play the power forward position. Redd led the state in assists. He can't shoot worth a damn, but he can pass the rock. He's only 5'4 and can dunk a basketball. It's one of the most amazing things I've ever seen in my life. His jumping ability is unreal. I filmed him dunking and uploaded the video on YouTube. During the first week, it gained 800,000 views. That's how he got noticed, good colleges. We've been cool ever since, that's when we became good friends. Now the whole world calls him by his last name, Redd. I met my other friend William Brown on the football field. He led State in our freshman year in total sacks at defensive end, 6'5 and 240lbs. The boy is huge to be in high school, a grown man. Last year, he put a hit on a quarterback that ended the guys› football career. The hit was vicious, paralyzed him from the waist down for the rest of his life. When we're in class and he's mad about something, you can see his muscle bulge like the Hulk. He mainly sleeps in the back of the room, so it›s hard to piss him off. The bad part is he snores loud. One time, he slept for five periods straight, we thought he was hibernating. He looked like an enormous grizzly bear. That's why we started calling him Bear. After being startled, I swiftly pulled my hand away. I didn't want the teacher to think I was cheating because I was passing a note to Kim. One of the officers was black and the other was white, and it didn't look like the mesh together. They walked over to the teacher's desk. She led them back out into the hall. They were taking their time talking about something serious or taking our teacher to jail. I told Kim to stop pulling my hair. I was getting frustrated because I was trying to focus on the police. It was already hard enough to hear with the door closed. Redd is the class clown, so he's brave. When our teacher leaves the room, almost every occasion, he'll pretend to teach the class. When he got up from his seat, I thought he was going to do his thang as usual. Instead, he crept over to the door, listening. Good, I knew he would fill me in on the details later. I tried to get his attention, and he waved his hand at me, signaling to be quiet. Suddenly, I saw his eyes pop out his head like a fish. If there is one thing I'm most certain of is he definitely looked at me when he said, run. He was loud enough to wake Bear out of hibernation. When the officers returned to the room, something told me to move fast and get the hell out of the classroom. The black officer called out my name. "Mr. Simmons." I hopped up, going with my first instinct. They walked over cautiously and tried to corner me. Suddenly, Bear speared the white officer. I know he hates the police, but damn. I didn't think he hated them enough to do that for me. That's my guy. I was on rocket speed, leaving the classroom. I hit the hallway, and my 4.3 turned into a 4.1 on speed boost. I could've beat Smoke. I hit the front lobby, where a dozen other cops waited for me... with guns.

Chapter 5
OFFICER DOWN

The black officer put me in the back of a police car. They repeatedly said a teacher had been murdered, beaten to death with a baseball bat. I pray no one believes I had anything to do with killing a teacher. Me, choosing to go to jail? Hell, no. I'm only sixteen years old. I still need to finish high school and you all want me to go to jail. Hell no, forget about it, I have better things than to be locked away like an animal. The first thing on my mind, call my father when I can get to a phone. He knows a lot of people in high places, and I'm sure one of them can help with this situation. I didn't want to get paranoid and look guilty, so on the ride to the detention center, I just sat back and relaxed. That's where they're taking me because I'm under young. I have to be seventeen to be sent to the county jail. They made all kinds of accusations and kept asking questions I couldn't answer on the ride over. I already knew what was up.

My father told me, white men want to rule the world, and they'll do anything to put a black man behind bars. They feel like we're a threat to takeover. To gain control over us, they have to lock us up and throw away the key. They're not about to throw away my key. We arrived at the detention center. They took me to a room with a table and four chairs. They tried to make me confess to the murder. I wasn't saying a word, the more you talk, the more shit you have to find yourself out of, I won't let that happen to me. They asked, why did I pick a baseball bat as the murder weapon. I don't know where that came from, but I didn't kill anybody. The officers were persistent about getting a confession. They thought I would tell on myself, that's right. I'm young and dumb. I don't know any better, help me. Yeah, I'm smarter than you think. I told them to talk to my lawyer. That's right, sucka. Talk to my lawyer. And by the way... I need my phone call. That's one thing my father taught me. If I ever went to jail, don't let anyone talk you into telling on yourself. Your lawyer should be the first person that comes to mind. Always have representation speak on your behalf. The less you say, the more you have control. I could tell they were getting frustrated. The black officer spoke, "We know it was you. We have your prints all over the weapon. Just make it easy on yourself and tell us what we want to know. We'll cut you a good deal." I saw the look on his face. His expression told me everything he said was bullshit. I knew he was lying. Keyword in that sentence, tell. Tell you what? That I did it so you can throw me under the jail. My father said, watch what goes on around you, and most importantly, people will lie to you, so learn their movements and expressions, and pay close attention to their actions. You'll be able to see the lie before it's told. A good deal would be clear of all charges because I'm innocent. I sat back and listened to them go on and on. The white officer finally gave up. I saw it on his face. He was more than likely tired and getting pissed at me. The black cop gave up a moment later. He said some harsh words to me before he left the room. I heard him say, black people are all the same and when you go to prison, you'll meet the best kind. Whatever, tell that bullshit to somebody who cares. I'm not planning on going to prison. Now that's settled, I need that phone call. I was left in the room by myself for a very long time. They probably thought I would crack after being alone, listening to my thoughts. That wasn't going to push me to the edge, and I don't mind being lonely. I need a clear head. Some other things were on my mind. Like, who in the hell took my baseball bat from my locker? Besides Kim, nobody else knew the combination. She's the only person who knows the code. When we break in between classes, she'll slip in notes and put girl stuff in my locker. Lunch is after the third period and we eat together every day. After lunch, she walks with me to my locker. Then, we'll walk to fourth period. That's our daily routine. I saw my bat the last time I opened the locker. The only other person that comes to mind is... my brother. He also knows the combination.

Chapter 6
BIG BUSINESS

I finally had a chance to talk to my father. He said, try not to worry. This will be over soon. The best lawyer in the country is on own our side. I took what he said into consideration. I trust my father. I won't drive myself crazy thinking about a crime I didn't commit. My father doesn't make promises he can't keep. When he wants something done, it gets done. Everybody respects him. He's not the Jamaican you want to test your luck. Money, power, and respect. He said that is what kept him alive for so long. I heard someone tap on the window. I turned around and saw the black officer swirling his finger in a circular motion, signaling to wrap it up. I sighed. The phone call was over, time to play the waiting game. He took me to another room, where I had to wait. The holding cell was small and ten other kids were waiting to be processed. One of the boys sat close to me. He smelt terrible. Maybe he took a shit on himself.

I moved away from him in a hurry. I would rather sit on the floor than next to a person who smells like shit. After I got away from him, I checked the playing field. I'm taller and have more muscle than most of the boys in the cell. I saw two boys around the same height as me. The others were a lot shorter. Another boy walked over and sat next to me. What was going on, do I look that friendly? He told me his name is T-Mac. I found out he's from Atlanta. He seemed like a cool person, so I decided to have a conversation. "What's your name?" He asked. I looked him over before I answered. You don't want to get to know just anybody. "Kane," I told him. "Kane, that's a cool name." He relaxed. "What are you here for?" "I rather not talk about it," I wasn't ready to tell him my personal information. "Not to be mean or anything, but I don't know you like that." I noticed a huge kid picking on a small, frail-looking boy. "Where are you from?" He asked. "If you don't mind telling me that." I didn't mind letting him know where I'm from. "Gwinnett County." I was still watching the bully pick on the other boy when I spoke. T-Mac saw me eyeing the kid. "Big Bruce." He told me. "Big Bruce," I responded. The bully grabbed the boy by the shirt. "That's him," He secretly pointed to the big kid. "Right there picking on that boy. He's sixteen and a real bitch. He kicked the principal ass, that's why he's locked up. Stay away from him. He's undefeated at our school." Damn, Big Bruce might be a problem.

I'm a nice size and can hold my own, and nobody would question my toughness. "Really," I assured him. "I'm not worried about Big Bruce." T-Mac is small and looks scary. Big Bruce probably whopped his ass a few times. I didn't want to think about fighting, so I changed the subject. "What are you here for, T… Mac?" "Gun," He answered without any hesitation. "Why did you need a gun?" I asked him straight up. Big Bruce yelled at the helpless kid and jerked him around like a rag doll. "Not just a gun," He said. "I brought a submachine gun to school." What the fuck, he took a submachine gun to school. Black kids don't carry semi-automatic weapons to school, that slot reserve for a special kind of breed. I glanced at him. He was paying attention to Big Bruce. "Why did you do something that stupid?" I had to know. I didn't imagine meeting a school shooter. "I'm guessing you didn't kill anybody, or you wouldn't be here with me. You'll be dead. Simple answer if you ask me." "Most people think it's a simple answer." He told me. "We're crazy, that's their assumption with kids like us. Well, it's not that simple. I have to defend myself every day from assholes thinking they can bully me. What is the use of having lunch money you won't be able to spend? Or… someone making fun of the way you dress. I was tired of it. The bullying had to stop. I tried to convince myself not to, but… as you can see." He paused for a moment. "I didn't only do it for myself. I did it for other kids in similar situations." "Big Bruce?"

I asked. "That's right," He answered. "I decided it would happen in the lunchroom. I wasn't trying to hurt anybody, only him. He was supposed to die today. That's one lucky sonofvabitch. Now, look at him over there bullying another kid. I fucking hate that punk." I've concluded that T-Mac is crazy. Before I could respond, Big Bruce punched the boy in the face hard enough to put him to sleep. Yeah, Big Bruce might be a problem.

Chapter 7
BIG BRUCE

I've gained weight and muscle since being incarcerated. I started working out three times a day and eating more. I'm huge, 6'4, and a solid 235lbs. I've been locked up a full year in the detention center. They are transporting me to the county jail where I will stand trial as an adult. I spent my seventieth birthday, incarcerated. Christmas, Thanksgiving, New Years, and even Halloween, were the worst. I felt lonely for the first time in my life. The only thing that got me through harsh times was when I had visitation. My parents came to visit when they could, and so did my boys after school. Smoke won another state title in the forty. Redd sat out for the entire basketball season, he dunked on a center and came down wrong. He broke his leg. It was the first play in our home opener. I can't imagine how he felt after missing the entire season. Bear was dropped from the football team because he slept too much in class. His grades fell and he got booted. My girl visited every weekend. She's my rock. The only other person I care about who didn't visit was my brother. My mother said he was studying, spending most of his time focusing on school. Right, I bet he was studying his ass off. Abel didn't want to look me in the face because I know his little secret. He murdered that teacher with my bat. I spent a lot of time thinking about it. I'll never say anything to anybody. I won't snitch on my brother like that. He's my brother and our mother thinks highly of him because he's smart. He's a momma's boy and something like that would crush her. It's not about how he handled the situation. I love my mother, so his secret is safe. That also meant not telling my father. The bus stopped in the back of the jail. We were all chained together as we exited in a straight line. We had to wait in a holding cell while being booked into the new jail. The cell smelled of musk all night. It was pure torture. Finally, I moved to the population in B-Block. I was unpacking when I heard a familiar voice. It was T-Mac. I haven't seen him since we got separated on the second day. T-Mac had been working out, I can tell. He's bulked up a bit. "Kane, that's you?" He sounded uncertain. "Yeah," I assured him. "T-Mac, right?" "Yeah, you still remember my name." He seemed excited to be my roommate. "I'm good with faces and names," I told him coolly. "It looks like we're going to be roommates." We finished unpacking and made our beds. We talked about his case. He said when he shot up the lunchroom. Seven people were injured. They didn't die but needed to go to a hospital for medical treatment. They booked him for attempted murder with a deadly weapon on school grounds. I finally told him what I was in for and he couldn't believe the situation. T-Mac thought I was innocent. I avoided speaking about my brother. I did mention it was a setup. We walked to the wreck-yard, everybody stayed within their own kind. The blacks were playing ball or in groups freestyling. White people smoked the most cigarettes. All they did was chat in small groups throughout the yard. The Hispanics were against the wall in a line. A few of them played volleyball when it was nothing else to do. People segregated, I didn't want to chill with anybody, so I found my own spot. My father taught me, people who separate themselves from their race, won't win. Now, I know what he meant. The middle of the yard was open. A huge freaking black dude walked out to the center. He looked about 6'7 and 250lbs of solid muscle. He stopped. Something was about to go down. The basketball accidentally hit his chest. He picked up the ball, that's when I finally got a good look at his face. Fucking, Big Bruce. He kicked the ball over the wall, then mugged the inmates standing on the court. I can't believe he pounded on his chest. This dude is vicious. The guys who were playing basketball looked scared. They wanted no smoke. Big Bruce just established himself as the bully in B-Block. The last six months were crazy. I hate to admit, but I'm getting used to being in jail. It's been a year and a half since I touched the streets. I lay back on my bunk at night and think about all my friends, family, and most of all, Kim. Sometimes I wonder if I'll ever see them again outside of this place. I think about everything I want to do now. +9It's messed up what happened, all the things I could've done, my dream of playing football in the NFL. I talked to a few inmates who said I shouldn't worry because my family has money. Here, money doesn't mean squat. You can't rock the latest fashions. You have an old dusty jumpsuit, no Jordan's, jewelry, or technology. It's hell. I stay in one building all day. It's supposed to be a college dorm room. Once you're in the system, they have you forever. My father runs a business. I don't. I'll work for him in the end. I don't want to be a desk worker. That's not me, behind a desk? Hell no, I wouldn't know the first thing about running a business. I just want to play ball. I started to gain hope when my lawyer said he could use the videotape from the hallway at school during the time of the murder. The footage will show me walking to class, as I claimed. The only thing I need to happen is the judge to approve the tapes. My lawyer said I should be good. I try not to think about it. I just need it to happen. "Kane," T-Mac called my name. "It's breakfast time." "I'm up," I told him. "Just thinking about life." I got out of bed to brush my teeth. "You already know it's the weekend." I saw him sit up and grab his stomach. "Oatmeal and cereal, my favorite." He hopped down from his bunk. T-Mac loves oatmeal and cereal. I've never met anybody who wants it more than him. I guess jail will do that to you. We waited for the deputy to call our room number. T-Mac waits with his hand on the doorknob so he can quickly get to the stairs. He wants to be the first person in line. He lifts a chair to save me a seat, that's love because I never have to rush. The deputy called our room number and T-Mac shot out the room like a cannonball. I took my time. I finally got my food after waiting in a line that wrapped around the room. I searched for T-Mac. He was sitting close to the TV area, I walked over and before I could sit down. Big Bruce sat down first. I looked at T-Mac and he just shrugged. Well, he did beat me to the seat. I wasn't about to fight him over a chair. The hell with it, I found another seat at the table across from them. T-Mac tried to get up, and I heard Big Bruce say, sit the fuck down. I saw the look on T-Mac's face and he didn't want trouble. I felt the need to say something. I didn't want to look like his protector. Big Bruce reached his enormous hand over to T-Mac's tray and grabbed his cereal. T-Mac sat there, reluctant to defend himself. Big Bruce is a cereal bully and he doesn't care who knows. I watched that big bastard take cereal from everyone sitting at the table. Three grown men did nothing, fuck Big Bruce. I got up and grabbed T-Mac's cereal and tossed it back on his tray. Big Bruce's face turned red as a crayon and he immediately stood up from his seat. A gut feeling said punch him in the face, and I did, it was an excellent straight hand to the jaw. He stumbled back, then rushed at me. I caught him as his arms wrapped around my waist. Inmates were shouting, fight. He was stronger than I thought. I tried to knee his face but was unsuccessful. He lifted me off my feet. His upper body strength was incredible and I was slammed down hard on the table. Milk, cereal, and oatmeal splashed on everyone. I was still down on my back when my hand found a tray. I smacked Big Bruce over his enormous skull. The force behind the blow brought him down on one knee. I pushed off the table and kicked him in the face. He spit blood in the air like a slow-motion action scene. I stomped his face in the ground like my life depended on it, blood covered his face, which didn't give me a reason to stop. Suddenly, I got hit in the back and I fell forward to the ground. I felt electricity all over my body. The goon squad had rushed the block with taser guns. They dragged us by our feet to the hole. It's a small dark cell without any windows at the bottom of the jail. I heard the inmates cheering my name as we left the block. "Kane! Kane! Kane!"

Chapter 8
KEY PLAYER

Jar was back in the United States from Africa. It's been two weeks since he's been home. He hated being away from his family. Especially his wife. The flight back felt like forever. He couldn't wait to get home. He didn't get the chance to talk on the phone much with Noti. He had to take care of several business moves while visiting the country. There wasn't time for anything else, or he would be jeopardizing his business and family. He had to be focused all the time. The black notebook was still inside his briefcase. His darkest secrets were in the book, and no one has ever read it. He keeps it secure in a safe in his office. If the book ever fell into the wrong hands, it could destroy his family. The plane finally landed, and the limousine had arrived. He entered the limo and gave directions to the driver. He decided to stop by the office before heading home. He had some old paperwork work to finish and still had to put away the notebook. The limo arrived at the office. Jar thanked the driver before he got out of the vehicle. He entered the building and said hello to the assistant at the front desk. She smiled. He walked into his office and cut on the lights. Everything looked to be in place. He went to the closet and hung up his coat. There was a secret door in the back and he slid it sideways. The space had just enough room to hide a small safe inside the wall. He put in the combination and it clicked open. He opened the briefcase and grabbed the black notebook. He placed it inside and locked the safe, slid the door shut, and left the closet. He sat down at his desk and unpinned his dreads to let his hair breathe. He figured he would knock out the paperwork and return some messages. His assistant brought in a fresh cup of hot coffee before she left the room, he thanked her. He blew over the steam, took a sip, and then pressed the play button on the answering machine. The last message took his breath away every single time he played it. For two years, his son's voice didn't get old. Dad, I'm being held at the detention center. I need your help. I was arrested for murder.

Chapter 9
REMEMBER ME

"It's over," A harsh voice spoke. Jar felt a brutal blow to the back of his head. His legs buckled and he fell to the ground. Somehow, he gathered the strength to roll over onto his back. He couldn't see a thing, everything in view was blurry. He held the back of his head. The feeling of blood leaking through his fingers didn't feel so good. His eyesight regained focus and he was able to see his assailant. "You," He groaned in agony. "I always knew it would be you." The gunman stood firm over Jar and pressed the gun to his face. "I guess you were correct about something for the first time in your despicable life." He smirked. "Please," Jar pleaded for his life. "Don't do this-" He was interrupted. The gunman fired two shots in Jar's face. Large chunks of his head erupted like tiny volcanos filled with blood. The gun exploded a second time. His entire body jerked as if each bullet was a volt of electricity. Three large sections of his suit jacket had disintegrated into the air. His chest settled as his breathing stopped. Abel stepped over Jar's lifeless body. "You were a bad father." He looked around the office. The old man was a part of something big that made their family very rich. His father traveled out of the country more than a celebrity. He was in real estate and they were considered wealthy. They live in a mansion, own expensive cars, and could afford a year around maid. Jar had the money to buy whatever he wanted without any problems. "Where the fuck did you hide it, old man?" Abel sat down at the desk. He needed to relax for a moment, clear his head of what he just did, killing someone was that easy. He leaned back in the chair and began massaging his head. He was the only man in the family with a baldhead, Kane and his father have dreadlocks. He thought their hairstyle looked disgusting and nappy. A baldhead is a sign of power, and that's what he desired most, the impact on making important decisions. He removed a cigarette from behind his ear. He fired it up and puffed out rings of smoke. He stared at his father lying on the floor, dead. He smiled. When he was eight years old, he got bitched at for smoking. He had found one of his mother's cigarettes and smoked it in the backyard. His father caught him red handed and gave him a long speech about smoking at a young age. He was addicted to cigarettes because they helped him think. One of the reasons he got through college in his freshman year. He put out the cigarette bud on the desk and walked over to his father. He crouched down next to the body and placed his hand on his forehead. He closed his eyes and sighed, ready to speak to the dead man. "Where do I have to look, old man." His fingers were touching Jar's forehead as if he was pulling memories from his brain and receiving them into his mind. He opened his eyes and the closet stood out in his face. He grinned. "Thanks, old man." He walked over to the closet and opened the door. Everything appeared normal. There wasn't anything usual inside, a few suit jackets and a pair of pressed dress pants. "Decoys," He muttered. He moved the clothes to the side out of his way. He searched the top and bottom inner area at the back of the closet. He pulled the carpet back and didn't see anything suspicious. He carefully put it back in place. Before finishing, he spotted a crack running along the side. He thought it was odd, but continued laying the carpet. He placed the palm of his hand on the wall and knocked on the surface. Hollow, he thought. He glided his hand along the wall. Finally, he tried pressing and sliding his hands sideways in one motion. A hidden safe miraculously appeared behind the wall in a small space. He smirked. He tried a few combinations. Nothing. He thought for a moment, then entered their birthday. The safe popped open, revealing a black notebook. He smiled devilishly, "Thank you."

Chapter 10
GONE BABY -KANE-

I was arrested in November, two years ago. I spent the first year in the detention center and the second in the county jail. The judge finally gave me a court date on the last day of the court calendar. I got lucky. On the ride over to the courthouse. The only thing I thought about was coming home. My lawyer had done a damn good job acquiring the videotape. He watched the tape and said the evidence was clear. I was walking to class with Kim. Five minutes later, another person in a mask approached my locker, opened it, and grabbed the bat. That sounds damn good to me. The judge will have to view the tape. Once that happens, I should be set free. That's the way my lawyer explained it to me. This is my second chance, value your freedom. Starting all over is going to be hard. I don't know if I want to return to school. I'm about to turn eighteen. I'd look like a fool if I went back, the biggest 10th grader ever. Other kids will call me dumb behind my back because of my age. In jail, I'm the king. I whooped Big Bruce ass and they respect me for it. In school, I won't get any respect. The bus stopped in front of the courthouse. We all stood up to get off. It was hard to move because the guy I'm chained to is half my size. For every step I took, he had to take five. We finally made it inside the courtroom, and the guards lined us up, directing us to the first row. I sat in the very front. I turned around searching for my father and he was nowhere in the courtroom. The room was small and there weren't many people. My father had shown up to all my court appearances, but he wasn't here today. I checked a second time. Maybe he was still working or stuck in a meeting. I didn't want to worry. Although, he said he wouldn't miss today. Five other inmates saw the judge before it was my turn. I'm... kind of paranoid. The judge came down hard on all of them. The first guy got a sentence of five years for drug charges. The second, ten years for assault. The third, fifteen for assault and battery. The fourth, twenty for a home invasion. The fifth inmate sentence gave me the chills, forty years for murder. What the fuck, I can't do forty years If I lose this case. I'll die without my freedom. I was patiently waiting for my father to show. It was my turn to appear in front of the judge. I have to do this without my father. It will be hard without him. My lawyer presented the videotape as new evidence and the judge allowed the footage. After watching it for the first time, there is no way in hell I'm guilty. What my lawyer said would happen, happened. I walked to my locker with Kim. A person in a mask approached moments after we left, it was my brother. There shouldn't be any reason to believe the person in the mask was me. I walked off, case closed. My lawyer asked if anyone else knew the combination. I answered swiftly, no. Then, I thought about my brother. I could've given him up, but why? Family stuck together, right. If I went down for this, I still wouldn't give him up. What he did was unforgivable, something I will never forget. Still, I love him. He's blood. I looked at the crowd of people behind me after the video cut, then back at the judge. I didn't expect to see my father, but his assurance would've been good. The judge came to a decision. I've been waiting for this day to come. This is it and I took a deep breath with my eyes close. My life depends on the judge's decision. "Not guilty," the judge's voice cut through my thoughts. I heard the mallet bang and it sounded beautiful. I pumped my fist in the air. "Yes," I scanned the crowd one more time. My father was nowhere to be found.

Chapter 11
WELCOME HOME KANE

When the judge said not guilty, I could've cried. I just got my life back. I wanted my father to be here so he could hear the judge say those words. This isn't about me winning, we did it together. My father said we were in this together. He did everything in his power to clear my name. I thought he was the one on trial. I still find it odd my he wasn't in the courtroom. I'll call him when I get back to the other jail. Since I was proven not guilty, my lawyer requested that I'm released immediately. My ride back to jail was different, an officer drove me in a squad car, and I wasn't handcuffed. This is much better than being chained up to another person. I kept my mouth shut for the entire ride. I didn't say anything to the officer. After thinking about it, he looks like the officer who arrested me two years ago at school. He kept looking at me through the rearview mirror suspiciously. Maybe he is the guy. I turned my attention out the window watching life. Hell, watching everything we passed by in the free world. I can't wait to eat some real food. Jail food is nasty. My mother can cook when she wants to. Occasionally she'll prepare a family dinner when my father returned home from long trips. Thinking about her food made my stomach growl. I miss it. I asked my mother to open a restaurant, and she gave me a crazy look, she never had a job in her life. My parents moved from Jamaica two years before we were born, she said it was for the better. Our future was in the United States. I thought about my boy T-Mac and how we became good friends. I'll leave him my information so he can keep me posted on his situation. I hate to think about Big Bruce. I know something will go down between him and T-Mac. Especially if I'm not around to save him. He'll never forget our fight. He wants revenge. The officer turned up the volume on the radio, interrupting my glorious thoughts of freedom. I overheard the dispatch say, all units need to report to 8785 Mills Dr. I didn't hear that right, that's the address of my father's office. I focused on the radio, listening carefully to everything the women said. There's been a murder at 8785 Mills Dr. We need all units in the area. I heard correctly, that's his office. I began to worry, a murder. I hope he's ok. This could be the reason he didn't show in court today. I caught the officer's eyes in the rearview mirror. He was looking at me strangely. His demeanor changed after the dispatch spoke on the radio. You can tell when a person doesn't like you. That's how I feel at this very moment. I can't think about his feelings. My main concern is my father. I know every single person at the office, it was about eight people working there two years ago. I have to consider that more people work in the building as time passed. That leaves me with only one question if he is the victim. Why would someone want to kill my father?

Chapter 12
AGENT JORDAN

It was a long meeting at the office today. I've been working for the Federal Bureau of Investigation for seven years. I wanted to be a cop ever since I played cops and robbers when I was little, holding a plastic cap gun and busting bad guys. Criminals try to anticipate an officer's next move, but always fail to realize when the heat came down on them. That's the fascinating part about this line of work, being a tough guy. I love having my pistol at the ready and shouting, police, get down! My team, putting those fuckers down. There is nothing like watching their confused facial expressions when they're in custody. I don't feel bad for anybody I brought to justice. I was glad to leave the department as I walked to my car. I opened the door and tossed a file folder on the passenger seat. The information inside the folder covers the African Black diamond, a new case I have to work because the Africans were making threats. I got in, closed the door, and started my Benz coupe. The motor sounded amazing. I take pride in my car because I worked my ass off to afford something I consider high-end. My phone buzzed. It was my new partner, Rick. He's new to the system and looks like a corny white boy you wouldn't have paid attention to in high school. I'll have to show him the ropes just like any other rookie. Joining the FBI is nothing like being a regular cop. We pursue top of the line criminals. Nothing's sweet. You have to be a tough sonofvagun, that's how I moved up so fast. To go undercover is to blend in with their kind, not be noticed. I have years of undercover experience. Your mind becomes someone else after being around mafia members who will murder you without question. It's a ton of pressure and some fold. The few who make it through, complete the mission. I was successful at completing four high profile cases in seven years. There was a stretch where I was undercover for two years infiltrating the largest drug empire in Atlanta. The Mafia Family, aka TMF. I have to stay low key for a while until things die down. Now I'm on the diamond case. Rick and I suppose to watch over it for the month. I have to keep my face off the streets. I flipped my phone open. "What's going on, Rick?" "Jordan, are you heading to the museum? I want to check the area before they bring in the diamond." Rick sounded ready to get to work. "Sure," I told him. "Where do you want to meet?" "Well, I'm still parked behind you at the department." He said. "We can ride together if you want?" I looked through my rearview mirror and tried not to be noticeable. Rick was on the phone, parked behind me as he had said. He probably looks at me as his mentor. I'm not that person, kid. I felt weird and didn't respond. "Jordan, you still there?" I heard Rick call my name, but I got lost in my thoughts for a moment. "Yes," I responded. "Your car or mines?" "We can take your car if that's ok with you?" He said. "I want to look at the file on the diamond on the way over to the museum." "That's fine with me, come on," I told him. I watched Rick through my rearview get out of his car. He approached my vehicle and I unlocked the door. I moved the folder off the seat so he could sit down. He had a file on the diamond, so I tossed my copy on the backseat. We both strapped on our seatbelts. The ride over to the museum didn't take long. I pushed the V-12 motor as we got on the highway. That's a certain level of freedom that comes with being an FBI agent. Rick, on the other hand, appeared to be paranoid. I told him to relax. We're above the law. I got us to the museum in no time. We went inside and checked out where the diamond will be displayed and all of the entrances. One hour later, we received a call ordering us to report to a high school. Someone murdered a teacher.

Chapter 13

A LONG ROAD

We arrived at the school in under twenty minutes. We got out and walked through the double doors in the front of the building. The chief of police and the principal greeted us at the door. We entered the classroom where the murder occurred. There was a woman slumped over on her desk with her head cracked open. This was a hate crime by the severe damage to her skull. Her brains are on the outside of her head, a gruesome crime scene, blood spilled from her head onto the desk. I hate to say it, but shit like this excites me. I'm a part of the action and that's better than watching a diamond all day in a boring museum. I walked around the desk and noted everything I saw. The majority of agents use a pen and pad for taking notes on a crime scene. Not me, I have a damn good memory. I looked over at Rick. I can tell he's never seen a body this bloody and brutally beaten. He looks sick to his stomach, and his face turned purple. I focused my attention on the dead teacher. I looked around the area and spotted something out of the ordinary. I got on my knees and cautiously lowered my head close enough to the floor to check out the object. It was exactly what I thought I saw, unbelievable. I slipped on a pair of latex gloves, then reached under the desk. As a detective, this is what you want a suspect to leave behind, evidence. What I have is a possible murder weapon. Whoever committed this crime knows how to swing a baseball bat. Rick didn't know how to handle the situation as a rookie agent, so I sent him to get the records from the lunchroom database. I had to explain that students don't only use cash to buy lunch. The school lunchroom system has an upgraded fingerprint payment method. He finally realized my great idea. If we can run all the prints from the lunch database, there's a slight chance we could find a match. Thank you, I know it's a highly creative idea. This is the kind of thinking ability you have to possess to be a top agent for the FBI. It didn't take long to match the prints on the bat with the database. The system gave us a name, Kane Simmons. That's the easy part, all we have to do now is arrest Kane while he's still in school. The principal gave us his information. He's in his fourth period classroom. Rick and I got the directions. It took two minutes to reach the location. We entered room 708 in the seven hundred hallway. There were about 25 kids in the class staring at us as if we were the bad guys. We're aliens to them. Young adults try to avoid the law until they get into trouble. All of the attention was on us. I felt a bad vibe in the air. After surveying the room, I easily noticed an enormous kid sleeping in the back with his head down on the desk. He had his own section. It's probably best if we left him alone. We approached the teacher and asked her to come into the hallway to speak in private. She complied and led the way out of the classroom. Once Rick shut the door, and we were all standing in the hall away from the kids. I explained everything to her in under five minutes. She opened the door, and we walked in on a skinny kid by the door, yelling out, run! Suddenly, a tall kid stood up as if we were coming after him. His chest was heaving, a sign that he was panicking. That was my cue. I used my calm voice when I called his name. "Mr. Simmons?" I stepped closer to Kane and paused, trying to appear harmless. That opened minded approach didn't work. I have a feeling Kane is about to run for his life. His facial expression told the story. He was scared. At that moment, I saw a fucking monster in the back of the room. It was that huge kid and he was wide awake. Something told me he was infuriated after being woken up by two guys who resembled officers. Surprisingly, the enormous kid rushed at me. I swiftly sidestepped, avoiding contact. He kept charging and connected with a powerful spear that sent Rick to the ground. Hopefully, that kid plays football. He could've been a great linebacker playing for the NFL, but he had to be dumb enough to assault an FBI agent. I wanted to help Rick, but Kane had run out of the room at an incredible velocity that I felt the wind as he shot passed. I hopped over Rick and the big kid before entering the hall in pursuit. Kane was moving down the hall at rocket speed. There wasn't any way I could catch him. He had to be moving at about twenty miles per hour. I'm too old for a race against young legs, so I had to improvise. I radioed the other agents in front of the school. I informed them a kid was running in their direction, apprehend the suspect at once. After I finished playing the hunting game, I went back into the classroom to check on Rick. My partner remained sprawled out on the floor. I cuffed the gigantic kid after the teacher calmed him down. He'll probably spend a night in jail. I helped Rick up, and he grunted as my extra hand hoisted him up from the floor. His face showed signs of agony as he stretched his lower back muscles. I heard him mutter. "I'm sure he's a football player."

Chapter 14
BACKSEAT DRIVER

Finally, Kane Simmons will go to trial after two years. Unfortunately, I have to show up to court. I was involved with his arrest, and of course, I want to see him go down. Damn it. He beat his teacher to death with a baseball bat. What do you do with a kid like that? Do you let him back out on the streets after severing for only two years, seriously? We have to start setting an example, starting with these kids today. People just can't go around killing other people when they're ready. When I was undercover, you had to be prepared at all times because mafia guys are unpredictable killers. You can hunt or be hunted, cowboys and Indians, cops and robbers, but nobody played mafia bosses and hitmen... except me. I shaved my face for the first time in a while. I want to look nice when I show up for court today. This is a big murder case for me, and I know this kid is guilty. I finished ironing my pants and turned on the TV to watch the news. The first few storylines were boring, and then my case made the headlines. KAN SIMMONS COURT APPOINT HEARING BEFORE TRIAL The reporter mentioned my name as the officer who apprehended the kid. Now I'm even more famous. I will never be able to go undercover again. Luckily, they didn't show my photo. That wouldn't go well with a few individuals I know who would take pleasure in killing me. After Kane is found guilty, I'll get another promotion. Sergeant sounds nice. I put on my clothes and grabbed a quick bite to eat. It took me three minutes to make a ham and cheese sandwich. Before I left the house, I locked the door. I started the Benz and sat there for a moment. Yeah, baby. That motor sounds good. I'm supposed to meet Rick at the courthouse. I still have a little over an hour to kill, so I made a quick stop at the department. I want to see how many people caught the news. They should be paying close attention to me because I'll be their boss soon. I parked the car curve side at the department and walked into the building. Nobody was watching the news. Whatever, they're probably mad I got another case under my belt. I even have Rick in a position to win. This will be the first victory under his belt. The diamond case was a warmup. We worked a small-time money laundering case that turned out to be much of nothing. I've been working in the office for the past four months, doing absolutely nothing. I was taken entirely out of the action. It could be the higher ups trying to stop me from rising through the ranks. Either way, they won't be able to stop this win. Kane Simmons is guilty. I decided to leave my car and take one of the undercover squad cars. I arrived inside the courtroom just in the nick of time for Kane to take the stand. I could barely recognize him after the two years spent in jail. He sure did use the time wisely. He's enormous, a grown man's body. He looks about two inches taller and very masculine. The prosecutor asked Kane a few questions about the day of the crime. Suddenly, his lawyer presented a videotape. That caught me off guard. What the hell is this about and not to mention, the damn judge allowed it. After watching the footage, I saw Kane and a female with a nice round ass walk away from his locker, I guess. I paid more attention to the girl's ass more than anything else, and hopefully, the judge did the same. A few seconds later, a male in a mask approached the locker and opened it without any problems. Ok, it wasn't him. The way that guy opened Kane's locker, told me he had something to do with it or knew who committed the crime. Just another bad guy I have to bust. Immediately after the video finished playing, the judge came to a decision. I have a feeling this case will get continued because of the evidence. I heard the judge shout. "Not guilty." "Not guilty!" I yelled loud enough to be heard by everyone in the courtroom. The judge banged down his mallet. I stormed out of the room, frustrated.

After gathering myself, I walked back into the building. Even though I was highly disappointed, Kane was to be driven back to jail in a squad car ordered by the judge. I freely accepted the offer. I want to study Kane a little on the drive back to the jail. He's a free man, but I still feel like he knows the culprit. Surprisingly, he acted normal as if he was never on trial or spent two years in a shit hole. I adjusted my rearview mirror, playing it cool while I watched him. I was interrupted by dispatch. All units report to 8785 Mills Dr. I turned up the volume on the radio. There's been a murder at 8785 Mills Dr. We need all units in the area. I don't know why, but I glanced at Kane through the rearview. His reaction shocked me. The dispatch caught his attention, and he caught mines... Gotcha.

Chapter 15
BODY AT 8785

After dropping the Kane off at the jail, I responded to the call at 8785 Mills Drive. I want to find out firsthand what got his attention. He went from relaxed to paranoid within seconds. What would be the reason for him to react that way after being in jail for two years? He possibly knows someone at that address. I can feel there is something different about this murder. I have to be involved, even though it may not require an officer of my caliber. I've been out of action long enough. It's time to do what I get paid to do, be a Special Agent. I phoned Rick after leaving the jailhouse. To my surprise, he was on his way to the scene of the crime. He got a head start because I offered to drop off Kane. I told Rick not to touch or move anything and don't allow anyone else. I have to examine the scene without flaws. That's the best way. Leave everything untouched. I have a great eye at finding things, and bad guys always made mistakes. You just have to be a good detective to find what they did wrong. I also told Rick to get a profile on the victim. The sooner, the better. That's one thing I can say he's good at, gathering information on a person. He was one of the best profilers at the training center, and his detective work is kind of good. I guess that's why the bureau wanted Rick added to the team. I started my Benz and didn't wait to hear the incredible sound of the motor settle my soul. I'm on a mission, and no one will take this case away from me. It's been too long, and I'm damn sure tired of office work. I punched in the directions on my GPS. The easiest route to the crime scene displayed on the screen. I had a couple of drug busts in that area awhile back, nothing on the level of TMF. I parked in front of the crime scene. I noticed an ambulance, police vehicles, and Rick's car. We are the only FBI agents. I got to the building in a hurry. The inside has a nice amount of space. A beautiful picture of a family caught my attention. I looked around. Everything seemed to be expensive, the front desk, chairs, the marble floor, and a massive statue of a golden lion in the center. I walked past an amazing living room area that had a coffee table with magazines on top and featured a sizeable curved television. I badge my way through the local police who were on the scene. A male officer gave me directions to the location where the crime was committed. I walked down a nice hallway and made a right at the end of the hall. I came to a door that read, Mr. Simmons. My mind was in another place at the time, and I dismissed the name. I slipped on latex gloves before grabbing the knob to enter the room. I opened the door and the first person in view was Rick. He was hovering over the body with a file folder in his hand. Two policemen were in the room with him. One officer was looking over the office space, and the other was attending to a real emotional woman sitting behind the office desk. She looks Jamaican, very beautiful, dreadlocks with strong facial features. I bet she's never worked a day in her life. Anyone could tell by the expensive looking jewelry she's wearing, this is probably her establishment. Rick and I greeted each other, and then he filled me in on what he knew about the situation. The Jamaican man on the floor with his face half gone and three bullet holes in his chest was Jar Simmons. The beautiful woman sitting behind the desk is his wife, Noti Simmons. He handed the file folder to me and elaborated on Jar's entire history in the United States. I looked down at the body and then at Rick. I was confused about the information in the folder. Jar looks at least sixty years old, but his record only shows the past twenty years. Rick must have read my mind because he said Jar moved from Jamaica around that time. Anything before that, we have to inform Jamaica and ask to receive it from their international public records. That does make some sense. There should be enough evidence to solve the case. If not, that would be something I'll probably consider to further my investigation. I opened the file folder on Jar Simmons and scanned through the pages. Rick was right about Jar, for the most part. Something caught my eye and I began to sweat. I stared at the photo for five minutes to make sure I wasn't losing my mind. Kane and Abel Simmons, sons of Jar Simmons.

Chapter 16
BROTHER TO BROTHER -KANE-

The cop escorted me back into the jail, where I waited in a holding cell for about an hour. I was allowed in my cell to grab all my personal belongings. I gave everything I had to T-Mac. He was sad to see me go after saying I'm his only friend. Nobody made him feel cool like me and had his back in a fight. I gave him my information and told him to call. He never had anyone put money on his books. My family has enough money, so that won't be a problem. He told me not to worry about Big Bruce beating on his head. He made up his mind to be a man and stand up to him like me. I just smiled at him. Big Bruce could beat him to death, but he doesn't care. He wants to be a man true to his word and not be a disappointment. It was time for T-Mac to stop acting so damn scary. I said a final goodbye to T-Mac. The deputy led me to the front of the building. A lady at the desk gave me my belongings from when I was processed in the system. Whoa, my shirt and pants were extra small. It would take a miracle to fit in the clothes. People will think I robbed a fifth grader for his school clothes. I'll look like a Jamaican Incredible Hulk. I don't have any need for the clothes so I slid them back to her and took only the necessary items I could use, my cell phone, watch, the key to my house, two state championship rings, and my necklace with a small picture of Kim inside of a locket. I asked the lady at the counter where I could use a phone. She pointed to a holding cell that had the door removed. I saw three phones inside. I thanked her before I walked away from the counter. The cell was empty, so I had privacy. I walked over to the middle booth on the wall and dialed my home number. No one answered the phone. I tried calling four more times. I got the same results. Damn, not a great start to my freedom. I need to speak to someone immediately. I hate being in this damn place. I don't want to lose my composure, but I need to know what in the hell happened at my father's office. There was a murder at his address, and I need to know who was killed. I became frustrated and worried to death at the same time. All I can do is pray that my father is ok. If something happened to him, I'd go crazy. Not to mention the impact it could have on my mother. I tried the house phone again and got the same result. Shit. I decided to call my friends to see if I could catch a ride with one of them to the house. Smoke is my best friend, so I dialed his number first. He said he was out of town at the moment visiting his sick grandmother. He was excited to hear I was set free. When he's back in town, he'll give me a call. Next, I tried Redd. He answered, but unfortunately, he was at the hospital getting his leg cast removed. Hopefully, he'll be able to continue playing basketball. I called Bear and his number was disconnected. I hit Redd again to find out if Bear got a new number. He gave it to me and Bear answered on the second ring. He was in therapy. What? In what world does Bear need treatment? He explained that he found out he has a sleeping disorder called Narcolepsy. Basically, a person falls asleep at uncontrollable times throughout the day. He was in a session with the therapist, and I didn't want to interrupt his learning or whatever session he had to complete. I called my girl, Kim. She connected the call and sounded excited to hear my voice. She offered to pick me up before I even ask. I told her cool, and fifteen minutes later, she arrived at the jail. A Lexus drove up, and Kim got out of the car. I remember when she drove a Honda Civic before I got arrested. This car was new. She greeted me with a warm hug and kissed me all over my face. When I was able to breathe again, I told her to drive to my house. We got there in twenty minutes. I was surprised to know my key still worked. We stepped inside the house, and I heard somebody crying from upstairs. I ran to the top of the staircase, hopping two steps at a time. The cries were coming from my mother's bedroom. I knocked, nothing. I opened the door, fuck it. This is my parent's room. I saw Abel sitting next to our mother. It's been a while since we were face to face. He had his arm around her, holding her close. He looked up at me and spoke two words that made my heart stopped... Father's dead.

Chapter 17
THE SPLIT

"Dead," I muttered as I dropped to my knees. I felt sick. The room began to orbit around my head. There was a tight feeling in my stomach. I wanted to throw up, but I hadn't eaten any food. I coughed on my words as I tried to speak. My mother's cries slowly faded. She had a vacant stare in her eyes. My mind, body, and soul suddenly ached. This is a new type of pain I'm feeling, nothing is comparable. Am I having a mental breakdown? I tried to speak again, it transpired as an loud yell. I had to let my emotions run free. I wanted to die and I didn't know why. I just did. My entire life revolved around my father. I was always by his side, he's my hero. I never wanted to be like anybody else but him. You can name someone on TV or in sports, and I'll say no, I want to be Jar Simmons. My father, the great man who moved his family from the poorest city in Jamaica. He was a successful businessman from another country, living in America with wife and kids, who never worked a day in their lives, and now he's dead. I kept my hands over my face. I couldn't move any part of my body. My mind was unable to process the situation. This is what it feels like to be in shock. A soft hand gently touched my shoulder, bringing me back to reality. I stood up from the floor. Kim embraced me in her arms. Tears began to slowly stream down my face. I couldn't cry in front of her, not like this, but I didn't have a choice. My emotions were all over the place. I held her tight, and her body felt soft and warm. Her head caressed against my chest. I reluctantly pull away, her eyes were watery from crying, she could feel my pain. I gave her another hug and kissed her on the forehead. Then I turned my attention to my family. When my mother looked at me, she began to cry with even more emotion. It didn't cross my mind at first, but maybe because I look exactly like my father. I sighed and glanced at Abel. He didn't appear affected by our father's death. I can't comprehend how he felt. What I do know is when we were growing up, he was never around us. He stayed with our mom all day. My brother isn't anything like dad. His emotions probably won't be the same as mines. I walked over to my amazing mother and sat next to her. Her hug was full of emotion. She's a strong woman, but I know she'll need her boys now that her husband is dead. The look on Abel's face made me skeptical about his feelings. I think my mind started playing tricks, or he was jealous because we hugged. My mother let me go and sadly said. "They killed him, Kane. Why did they do this to me?" She fell back into my arm, crying harder. I thought, they? Somebody wanted my father dead, but for what reason? I know very little about his business. He worked in real estate and had a privately owned office building. I'm not a detective, but I will find out who murdered him. I'm going to punish whoever did this when I catch them. It will be ten times worse than what they did to him. There is nothing in life I want more than revenge. I told my mother everything would be alright, and I'll find whoever did this to us. Abel suggested leaving it up to the police. What the hell does he know? This cold hearted sonofvabitch murdered his teacher. Now he's talking about leaving it up to the police. I told him no matter what, I'll find who killed him. If it were mom, he would've gone crazy trying to find her killer. I stood up from the bed. I need to check out my father's office. The answer to why he's dead could be there, so that's first on my list. Abel grabbed my arm as I began to walk out the door. I was full of anger and blanked out, and my fist crushed Abel's nose. The force behind the punch lifted him off his feet, propelling him backward before landing on the bed. He held his nose as blood spilled off his hands onto his clothes. The two years I spent incarcerated cost him a broken nose. I don't give a damn about how he felt anymore. He saw the look in my eyes. This wasn't about our father. This is about keeping a life changing secret for your ass, for never visiting and leaving me alone with a death sentence. I didn't need to say anything. He knew I figured it out, he killed his teacher. He groaned through his hands while holding his nose. My mother stood up and pushed me out of the room. I thought I saw the devil sitting on my parent's bed when I looked at Abel. My mother was crying hysterically. "Stop, don't do this now." Kim stepped out of the door, and before it shut in my face. I saw my brother smirk and lick the blood off his fingers.

Chapter 18
THE PLANNER

The Planner stood outside of the Atlanta Museum. He was staring at the building from across the street, thinking about how easy it would be to set the place on fire with everyone inside, men, women, and children. Shit, he hated the little snot nose fuckers. He smiled, thinking about innocent people on fire, trying to run out of a burning building. He'll be the one greeting them at the entrance with an AK-47, filling their bodies full of bullet holes and ending their ability to escape death. He gripped the gun hidden inside of his coat, then began walking over to the museum. He had to keep himself under control because, at any given moment, he could snap and open fire on everyone in sight. Evil thoughts took over his mind. It was hard to be one person. He could be calm one minute, then instantly become somebody you want to stay away from, a killer. He entered the museum and took a deep breath. He had to wash away his murderous minded thoughts before people started to drop dead. He held his composure in check, then continued walking through the museum. He completely forgot to take his hand off his gun. The people closest to him would notice his suspicious behavior. To avoid any attention, he smoothly removed his hand off the weapon. Blood had to recirculate through his hand because of how tightly he gripped the handle. He was trying to blend in by becoming an ordinary human being. Innocent people walked by harmlessly, looking at everything in the museum that pleased them. Little kids were gawking at everything their tiny eyes could see, taking in each artifact. Oh, the pleasure. He thought. The urge to kill someone was bad enough that he began to sweat. He focused his mind, getting back on track. The museum is part of a forthcoming mission. He's been studying how the building operated for two years. Every day he came with his gun tucked in his coat just in case things got ugly. There wasn't one day where he didn't desire to open fire and send every terrified person running out of fear. He walked around for a moment, feeling like a god. His ball cap was pulled down over his eyebrows just below the eyes. If he happened to snap, it would be hard for anyone to recognize his face. He stood in front of four old pictures. They appeared to be ancient paintings of past kings. This was only his millionth time standing in front of them. He picked different positions every time he came and acted like he was intrigued by something in the area. This time, it was picture day. In reality, he was watching the item across from the paintings next to the security guards. He came up with different ideas to steal it from a heavily secured glass case. He knew every single way out and into the museum. His reasoning for taking long walks around the building. He mapped out the entire floorplan in his mind before going home and drawing everything he saw from memory. His one dilemma, enter at night or day? Security was tight during the day compared to only two guards at night. The museum has a highly advanced security system. He would play different scenarios in his mind after each carefully thought out plan. He could come during the day and hold up the place with a bomb strapped around his chest or come at night and cat his way through the ventilation system. Eventually, he'll have to set off the alarm to get his treasure. The Planner turned around and bumped into a little girl. Her mother ran over as if she had been looking for her lost daughter. There was a worried mommy look on her face. He gripped his gun out of habit. He slowly released the firm grip he had on the handle. Damn, I can't be paranoid. He overheard the woman speaking to the little girl about running off without her. Then she turned her attention to him. "Sorry," She offered an apology. "She's always wandering off and getting into trouble." "Oh, it's not a problem." He said with irony. "You're right for getting on her for wandering off. You never know what can happen if she bumps into the wrong person." He looked down at the little girl and smiled sarcastically. She looked about five years old. "My name is Molly." The little girl was willingly ready to tell him her name. "Molly," He repeated while maintaining his one of a kind smile. "That's a cute name." He thought it was one of the dumbest names for a girl. Stupid little girls wandering off with names like Molly, Heather, Susan, Becky, are all, I'm going to get kidnapped names. Luckily, he wasn't into bothering children because this would've been an easy snatch. "Molly, that's my name, mister." She said in a cute voice. "What's your name?" "That's none of your business," Interrupted her mother. "You have to leave other people alone, Molly." "Oh, it's quite alright." He convincingly told her a lie. "My name is Paul." He would never give someone his real name. "Paul, Paul, Paul," She annoyingly repeated his name. "Mama, can we play with Paul?" "No, honey." She told her daughter. "Remember, we're in a hurry to pick up daddy from work. We have to leave now, say goodbye to Paul." "Ok, bye Paul. Mama said we can't play. We have to get daddy from work." She skipped off beside her mother. "Paul, Paul, Paul..." The Planner sucked his teeth. He wanted to blow out the little girl's brains. He visualized the attack in his mind. She gave him a fucking headache. He sighed, that was a close call. Somebody name Molly could've died. He got back to business and walked over to the prize. He looked through the glass case. A 50 million-dollar, African Black diamond was calling his name.

Chapter 19
BACK IN ACTION -JORDAN-

Rick gave me a damn good profile on Jar Simmons. I sat at my desk, reading over the file. It's enough information on the victim to start the investigation. I have a substantial number of individuals that I can interview. I can tell Jar was a brilliant man after reading his profile. He moved his family from Jamaica and became very successful in the real estate market. His wife never had a job in the United States. She's been a stay at home mom for the past twenty years. Their kids are well taken care of and attend a private school. They live in a costly mansion in a good neighborhood. How did he make so much money in twenty years without a college education? Now that I'm thinking about it, Kane had the most expensive lawyer in Atlanta represent him in a murder case. I should've thought about the lawyer at the time and investigated his family. Jar was easily making millions every year. Their home is worth five million, easy. They own a $350,000 Aston Martin, a custom $280,000 Corvette, and a $500,000 Ferrari that's on backorder. This man was the best poker player and wasn't on the police radar. He could've been a legit businessman living an honest life, but somebody wanted him dead. I'll probably start with the family, see what else I can dig up about his personal life. Maybe I can find out if they knew anybody else he may have had trouble with, it could be a gambling debt, and he owes somebody money. I'll check if any of his family members in Jamaica are rich and find out who his friends are. They might know something that could help. I need to get a list of all the employees who worked at his office so that I can interview them. What doesn't sit right with me is not one, but two murders, both close to Kane. A teacher had been beaten to death, and his father murdered in his office. Nothing is making sense, the teacher and Jar, how are the murders connected? Kane, I don't see any other reason. I think something is about to go down with this kid. I know that much from experience and being undercover. When you get a certain feeling, telling you to react, go with it. The majority of the time, your instincts are correct. That's what I trained myself to do, go with my first instincts. It might save your life. I skimmed through all the files on each of the family members. Noti Simmons moved from Jamaica with Jar. She took care of the house. He loved buying her expensive gifts. She didn't like to shop much, not an outside person. She has never been in trouble since coming to America. That's a good way to live. Kane was born seconds before his twin brother, Abel. Two years after their parents were married. Kane was a student athlete. He was good at basketball, football, and track. My first initial thought was, he didn't play soccer. I thought foreign people love playing soccer, don't kill me. He won two state championships on the track team, back to back years. I thought about how fast he ran two years ago when he disappeared down the hallway. I never had a chance. His speed is extraordinary. I placed Kane's profile picture next to his father's photo. They have the same facial features, eyes, nose, mouth, and the same dreadlock hairstyle. They would look like twins if it weren't for the age difference. I flipped the page. I was staring at Abel's profile picture. He was interesting, very different from Kane. He's intelligent, excelled in every class, and has been a straight A student since the first grade. He skipped two grades and finished high school ahead of schedule. He enrolled at Yale University when he was sixteen years old. Damn. This kid can be a fucking scientist if he wants to take that route. I focused on his picture and noticed he doesn't have the same facial features as Jar. He has a baldhead and his eyes looked empty and cold. He resembled a madman with power. I felt my hands quivering uncontrollably. The file began to shake, so I place the folder back on the desk.

His picture somehow sucked all my brainpower. I began to sweat and became intimidated by the eyes staring back at me as if he were present in the room. Suddenly, someone grabbed my shoulder, and I hopped up from my seat, scared to death.

Chapter 20
WHERE TO GO -KANE-

My mother was right to push me out of the room. Things could've gotten worse with Abel. I thought about waiting downstairs or in my bedroom. Abel was home from school, so staying around the house wouldn't help. Something is wrong with my brother's mind. He's smart, but there is something twisted with his behavior. I've put up with his shit for a long time, and a mental break from him would be good for my health. I walked to my room and grabbed a few of my personal belongings. My old clothes won't fit, so I didn't bother wasting any time looking through them. I grabbed two pairs of shoes, some stuff for my hygiene, and my favorite picture of my father with me in his office on my fifth birthday. I put the picture in my wallet and everything else in a backpack. Kim and I immediately left the house after I got my stuff. I tossed the bag in the backseat before getting in the car. I adjust the seat back so

I could rest. I closed my eyes to relax and thought about my next move, like somewhere to stay until Able went back to school. Kim started the car, then asked where I was going to stay, if not at home. I said drive somewhere while I think, maybe a shelter? I don't have any money, meaning I'm dead broke. I could ask my mother for some money, but I don't want to beg her for anything, it's not the time. She's in a tough situation, and her source of income came from my father. Abel will only piss me off if I saw his face. It would be tempting not to knock his head off his shoulders. That's how dangerous I felt while around him. I'm trying to avoid being a rotten apple by not causing any more drama. I'm Jar Simmons' oldest son. I'll figure out a way to make some money. Maybe start with something I never had to do in my entire life, look for a job. Kim drove to Krystal's fast food restaurant. I can't afford to eat and I was hungry. I let her know and she offered to buy the food. Cool, I wanted to order every item on the menu. Everything on the board looked delicious. My taste buds were out of control. I have to limit myself because I don't have a clue how much money she wants to spend. It's hard trying not to be greedy, jail had turned me into an eating machine. You have to eat what's in front of you to survive. The food in the real world is a pleasure to me after what I had to endure while confined. I scanned the menu and ordered four Krystal burgers and a fry. Kim had a crazy expression on her face when she looked at me. I thought I ordered too much food for a moment. She wasn't trying to spend that much money. Instead, she said I'm too big for only four Krystal burgers, and it wouldn't fill my big head. I smiled. She ordered ten more burgers with cheese and an extra-large fry. Hell yeah, I appreciate her for looking out on the food. I'm hungry enough to eat more than a pig. She ordered food for herself, and we drove around to the window. When we got the food, the smell made me want to tear up the bag and destroy the burgers. I reluctantly waited because I didn't want to be rude to my baby. Some people don't like to eat in their vehicles and would rather wait until they got home. I can respect that. I waited for two years, just to smell burgers. After driving five more minutes, we pulled into some very nice apartments. I don't know who lives here, so I kept quiet as we parked in front of the B building. The letter B reminded me of B-Block in jail. I could go without seeing the letter B for the rest of the year. Kim told me to grab the food and follow her. I did exactly what I was told. She grabbed the drinks and my bag from the backseat. I was still trying to figure out where she was taking me. I remained silent and went with the flow, hoping she didn't think I would stay with a stranger. She used a key to open the apartment door, B-222. We stepped inside, and she set the drinks down on the table along with her keys. I sat down after her, ready to demolish the food. Kim's apartment is beautiful. It's a lovely living space. She has a nice size flatscreen in the living room, and all of her furniture looks new. I saw a trophy case that contained all of her awards, mostly track and field trophies. There are also pictures of her wearing a track uniform standing next to her parents. There is a picture of Kim and I hugging, sitting on the table next to a flower pot. I remember when Smoke took that photo when we were at practice. My eyes studied the plant for a short moment. It didn't look normal to me. It's very colorful, budded and it smells funny. I didn't dwell on it for long. My main focus was on putting food in my stomach. Kim said I could live with her after we finished our food. That solves one of my problems. She sent a love letter every week until the day I was released from jail. I know in my heart she loves me without a doubt. Something like this really shouldn't be a surprise. I have the same unconditional love for her. Suddenly, she picked a bud from the strange plant and rolled it in some paper.

Chapter 21
TAKE ACTION -JORDAN-

I frantically sprang out of my seat. I swiftly turned around and drew my weapon. Ready to blow somebody's head off. I caught myself at the last second. It was Rick, staring at the end of my barrel. "Damn, you scared the hell out of me." Everyone in the office was watching us. I looked like a fool. I lowered my gun and put it back in the holster. Rick cautiously lowered his hands. His eyes were wide and they slowly became normal. The look on his face told me he was terrified. I was losing my mind. Abel's photo somehow sucked the energy out of my body. I had never felt anything like that in my life. "Are you ok?" He sounded relieved. "I thought you were about to kill me." I eased my butt back down in my seat. Rick walked around the desk and sat down. "Listen, you can't sneak up on a guy who's been undercover as long as I had. I could've blown off your head. Especially in this line of work. People's nerves are bad because they worked in the field for a long time. Just look around this place, and you'll see what I mean." I sighed out of frustration. "I'm sorry about that." Rick apologized. "Next time, I'll make sure to take the long way around." Rick started looking at what I had on my desk. It wasn't hard to notice the file folder and all the photos I had spread out of the Simmons. "I see you're ready to get started on the Simmons case." He said. "That's right," I elaborated. "It's been a long time since I had a good case that truly caught my attention. I've been dealing with an overwhelming amount of stress from staying in the office. The kid we busted two years ago, Kane." He nodded. "The man who was murdered is his father. We can prevent something from happening to this kid. Two murders in two years. His school teacher and then his father. I believe both murders were related to however, our real estate guy was making his money. I don't know how, but I can feel this is the right direction. Jar was a big spender. I know we need to keep an eye on Kane. His life could be in danger." "You think the suspect who murdered Jar will come for Kane?" Rick asked. I sighed and adjusted back my seat. "Not sure. I'm thinking more like he can get in the way of somebody, possibly after something." I explained. "This is my perspective. Kane was really close to his father. If someone wants to know something about Jar, they might track down his son. I'm not saying Kane knows something, or Jar was conducting illegal activity. I also think he might try to find out who killed his father." "There isn't much to know about this guy besides he got rich really fast. He has money, but you think there could be something else?" He asked with a confused look on his face. "Maybe," I said nonchalantly. "If there is, I'll figure it out and who committed the murder. When a man of his stature gets killed, there's something of great value at stake. There's a possibility the suspect found exactly what they were looking for. And that's what I need to find out." "I understand what direction you're heading in." He said. "I think you're right about Kane. Although, I think the teacher's murder has nothing to do with Jar's murder. We can tell by the video. The suspect was a kid. Completely unexpected, but we lost. I don't know how I missed Kane being Jar's son, good catch. If they did have a close relationship, our killer would come after Kane. That's if they're still looking for something, but don't dismiss that Jar could've been murdered because he had information on someone. Kane is the key to solving this case if we look at it from your perspective." "We can drop the teacher for now." I agreed. "And I don't want anyone else involved. I can handle this by myself." This wasn't a case for the FBI. People are murdered all the time. Kane beat me once, and I won't let it happen again. That's the only reason why I'm not content with this situation. I hate to lose. "I want in on this one." He said excitedly. "We can bust this case wide open." "Sure," I agreed to let him help work the case. When we join forces, good things happen. He's not that bad of a partner, and he's a good listener. Plus, I can get more things done. Two minds are better than one. I knew Rick was a good agent. He did a fantastic job working on the diamond case. He's one of the better agents at the bureau as a rookie. And that's saying a lot because I don't like giving people comments. "I can use an extra hand." "Yes," he said. "Where do you want to begin?" "Always start with the family," I told him. "It's best to find out what they know first. That shouldn't be hard since it's only three of them. From there, I guess check out Jar's office. We need to investigate everyone who works in the building. You never know, our killer could be one of them. Who didn't work that day will be important. Those individuals would be my first guess. If the killer worked on that particular day, they would have to continue working without being suspicious. That's difficult to do without the right head on your shoulders." I stood up and grabbed my coat off the chair. We left the department, ready to take action.

Chapter 22
HIGH TIMES LOVE -KANE-

Kim finished rolling the weed she picked from the plant. What the hell was she doing? I don't know anything about smoking marijuana. This is my first time seeing it up close. She used her fingers to break down the bud into smaller pieces. Then she rolled the weed in cigar paper. She grabbed a lighter off a wooden table in the living room. I thought about telling her to stop, but I'm not in any position to be her father. The smoke produced a strong odor over the food. I thought she had lost her mind because I didn't know this about her. She was experimenting with drugs. She glided over to the entertainment system under the TV. Bob Marley was now playing on the radio. I knew his music very well. My mother listened to him around the house when I was young. She began dancing, swaying back and forth, feeling the different sounds in the air. The odor became stronger every second. I definitely smelt a powerful type of fruit. I saw people on TV and in the streets smoking weed, but nobody directly around me. I wonder if she thinks I care? I've never used drugs in my life. My father wouldn't allow us to fall into that trap. Kim started dancing more seductive. She appeared to be in a trance. I couldn't focus on eating. My eyes were stuck. She turned around and caught me watching, I felt embarrassed. Her eyes were low and red. It didn't take much to realize she was high. She began to dance in my direction. For some odd reason, she looked seductive while high. She sat on my lap and started slowly grinding while holding on my shoulders. It felt great. I never had a lap dance. I was locked up for two years. The only entertainment like this was reading books. Now, I'm the guy in the story with a beautiful woman grinding on them. I can finally tell the difference, trust me. I felt my manhood getting bigger every time her ass rubbed against it. Oh, shit. I don't want her to feel my erection. She'll think I'm horny. I've never done it. I was locked up when teenagers just started thinking about sex. Kim is my girlfriend. What if she wants to have sex with me? I don't even know how to ask. She placed my hands on her butt, and it felt soft. I went with the flow and gripped her ass. This was getting better, shout out to my boys in county jail. They all could imagine being in this situation. She blew smoke in my face, and I could feel it entering my lungs. Suddenly, she opened my mouth with her lips. I thought she wanted a kiss. Instead, she blew smoke down my throat. It was unexpected and I began to cough. She told me to take it easy and then put the blunt to my lips. I played it cool as if I've done this type of thing before. I don't want her to think I'm lame. She knows everything about me, which includes never using drugs. I puffed on the blunt, and everything around became mellow. My body felt relaxed and chill. I focused on Kim. Her energy was feeding my soul. She lifted off her shirt and then unsnapped her bra. Oh man, this is about to happen. She wants to have sex. Her breasts were firm and the perfect size. She cupped both of them in my hands. Damn, I think being high was playing a part in how I felt. After a few minutes of touching, she got up and undid my pants and slid them down. I forgot I had an erection. It was standing straight up in her face. Wow. What she did next was surprising. The entire thing was in her mouth. It was an incredible sensation that lasted about five minutes. My legs began to twitch, and I felt a rush of blood starting at my feet. I came. She massaged my manhood, getting it hard a second time. She slid off her pants and got back on top. She moaned while grinding ferociously in my lap. I felt like a superhero with extraordinary strength. It was the best feeling I've ever felt in my life. It was very tight and wet. I'm large down there and I know she could feel it. I tried not to hurt her, but I couldn't help losing control. I thought she wanted to scream, but her movements became faster. She enjoyed every second. I saw the look on her face. I began to feel a pleasurable rush through my entire body. This was something new, and I wanted to destroy her insides. I started growling like an animal against her seductive moans. She pulled on the back of my hair. I watched her eyes roll back into her head. Finally, it was ending. I felt myself releasing inside her. Her vagina throbbed around my manhood. She started shaking and her breathing was intense. Suddenly, she relaxed into my arms. She said passionately. "Our first time."

Chapter 23

ABEL THE BALDHEAD GENIUS
-JORDAN-

Rick and I got in my car and left the department. We decided not to alarm the neighbors by taking a marked police vehicle to a high-end neighborhood. We wanted to avoid setting off any alarms. Rich people don't like trouble. This is my second murder case with Rick. When he saw the dead teacher, I thought he wouldn't make it at the bureau. Jar Simmons was different. Rick seemed a bit more comfortable being around the body. He was adjusting to seeing dead people. I'm not sure how he will react if we went head to head with a killer. The first case didn't involve a suspect who knew what they were after. It was a failure because we apprehended who we thought was the killer. The only evidence we had was Kane's fingerprint. After we took him into custody, the fieldwork was done. This will be our first thorough investigation. We got our game plan together on the way over to the Simmons residence. I went over questions to ask and not to ask. Rick will have to interview family members and other potential suspects. This won't be easy, like the training center. I need to make sure he doesn't make any rookie mistakes. I can't fuck this up. The Chief would be all over my ass. After I carefully went over the plan. He asked if he could interview one of the family members. If things go right, I might give him a chance. The main reason he's here is to watch my back. Just sit back, learn, and observe every detail. One day he'll get an opportunity to solve a murder case on his own. We drove up to an enormous house. I checked the GPS to make sure we were at the correct location. Their mansion was beautiful. The grass on the front lawn was the greenest I've ever seen. Well kept. An Aston Martin and a Corvette were parked in the front driveway. The two vehicles I read about in Jar's portfolio. I shut the motor off and turned to Rick. He looked anxious, so I told him I'll handle the questioning. He agreed and then we got out of the car. We walked to the front door and right before I was about to knock. It magically opened as if someone expected our arrival. The same eyes from the photo were staring at me, sucking the life out of my soul. It was the man with the baldhead. I felt like I couldn't breathe and became lost for words. I couldn't get out what I wanted to say. There was something scary about Abel that frightened me to death. I stood in the doorway, staring back at Abel. He had a confused look on his face. Suddenly, Rick spoke up when I couldn't, taking over the lead. He told Abel we were with the FBI and investigating the murder of his father. Abel turned his attention to Rick. I felt better because he wasn't staring at me. I felt trapped. It was hard to look him in the eyes. My body became weak, and I think he knew I was vulnerable. Rick told Abel we have a few questions. He stepped out of the house and shut the door. He's not as big as Kane, and I couldn't tell how they're twins. I know sometimes twins don't look the same. Abel has an entirely different persona. He was well dressed in slacks and a button up shirt. He wasn't wearing jewelry or gym shoes like his brother. He had a nice shaved face and smelt good. He even looked intelligent. I played the background while Rick went to work. He asked Abel if he knew anything about his father's business or anyone who wanted him dead. Abel answered no to most of our questions. Rick finally asked if his mother was home and if we could have a word with her. She was in the house, but not in any condition to speak. He told us to check back at a later time and date. She was still emotional over the death of her husband. Rick thanked Abel for his time before he went back inside. I sighed after he closed the door. I felt my energy returning in my body. Rick was back in the car when he called my name. I was unaware he had walked away. I was still facing the door. I snapped back into reality, happy to be out of Abel's presence.

Chapter 24
JOB HUNTING -KANE-

I woke up the next morning feeling amazing and ready to start the day. The bedsheets were still wrapped around my body. I turned over to face Kim, and she wasn't there, just a fluffy pillow. It's early, and she's gone. No worries, I stretched before I got up because my body felt stiff. I thought about what happened last night. We lost our virginity. It felt great because she's the woman I love, and she didn't have to wait for me. That's the wonderful part about being in love. I got up from the bed and realized it's one in the afternoon. Damn, I was behind on time. I had been asleep all morning. The bathroom was calling my name. Bad breath wakes up with everybody, and I need to take a hot shower. After I finished, I had to shave. The best way to get a job is to be clean. Who wants to work around a dirty person? I freshened up and left the bathroom with confidence. I heard the front door shut, followed by Kim shouting my name.

I walked out of the bedroom with a towel around my waist. She was carrying two shopping bags and set them on the floor. She gave me a hug and a passionate kiss on the lips. The bags were filled with a mixture of men's clothing. She took the opportunity to go shopping while I was asleep. She just kept surprising me. I told her, thank you. If I get an interview now, I'll look professional. I tried on the clothes and they were a perfect fit. She has a good taste for fashion. I'm used to wearing an orange jumpsuit. I didn't know what people were wearing. She said I look good and somebody would give me a job. That gave me even more confidence. She grabbed the bags and took them into the bedroom. Then she asked what I wanted to eat. I told her whatever she got a stomach for, surprise me. I'm not a picky eater, being in jail fixed that problem. I dressed in a pair of casual clothes. Kim made me a chicken sandwich. It was delicious, so I asked for another. After I ate, we left the apartment, and she took me to get my license. On the way, she gave me a lesson to help with passing the driving test. I have a pretty good memory. I used to meditate when I was locked up as a way to keep my mind strong. It also helps with your memory. We walked inside of the MVA, and the place was overcrowded. People were standing in extremely long lines. I had to get a ticket at the front desk and wait until that number was called. We waited for an hour. I heard my number and it appeared on the board. I went over everything Kim taught me in my head. I entered a small room with multiple computers inside for people to take the test. I picked a random seat and typed in my information. The test began, and everything Kim mentioned was on it. After I answered each question, it was complete. The screen displayed a passing grade of 90 percent. I wouldn't know how to tell Kim if I had failed. I went back to the desk to report my score. The lady said someone would call my name to take the road test. I had to wait ten more minutes before I heard my name. I used Kim's car. I successfully passed without any problems. The instructor told me someone would call me to take a picture ID. Damn, I have to wait again. I didn't think it would take this long to get a driver's license. I sat down next to Kim and told her I had to wait again. Finally, I took my picture. I didn't wait for the guy to say to me I had to wait. I just sat down. The MVA is almost worse than jail. It only took five minutes. I was relieved it was over. I couldn't wait another second without losing my mind. I approached the desk and finally received my license. The lady told me to make sure all the information was correct. I looked it over and it was right. I stared at my photo on the way back to Kim. My father was staring back at me, eighteen-year-old Jar Simmons, his younger version. We happily left the building. That was a grueling process. When we approached the car, she tossed me the keys. What? She wants me to drive. I've never driven a car for more than five blocks. Everywhere I went, my father drove. I took a deep breath and started the car. I reversed out of the parking space and pulled off. She told me I drive slower than old folks, and her grandma drove faster than me. I laughed, but I was trying to prevent an accident. I picked up speed as I got more comfortable. I felt less pressure when the instructor was in the passenger seat. I guess I feel different because it's her car. Everything went smoothly. I turned off the car and exhaled. I walked into a restaurant to get my first application. Ready to start job hunting.

Chapter 25
THE GAME

It's been a week, and I'm sitting around the house without a single job offer. Not getting a callback has been stressful. I was unaware finding a job would be this hard. I never had to go through this hard of a process. I even followed up by calling a few places where I put in an application. I basically got the same answer from everywhere I applied. Sorry, we're not hiring at the moment, or we'll give you a call when we're looking for help. I was beginning to think I wouldn't get a job. What I'm I going to do with myself? Kim told me to keep my head up and keep trying. I don't want to disappoint her, but damn. Everybody had said no, so far. It was going to be hard to tell her. I want her approval and not think of me as less of a man. I was staring at the number to the last place I put in an application. I was contemplating if I should call. I thought about it for a good ten minutes. If I don't call, I'll never know. I picked up the phone and dialed the number. A lady with a sweet voice answered the line. I told her who I was and why I was calling. She told me to hold while she got the manager. This is the furthest I've gotten on any of the calls. Maybe I can get an interview? I'm dying for an opportunity. She got back on the line. Her first two words, "We're not-" I just hung up the phone, cutting her off. Why listen to the rest? I already knew what she was about to say. I have to man-up and ask my mother for some money until something falls through. It's been a week since I spoke to my mom. The last time we were together, she pushed me out of her room. I wanted to give her some time after I had punched Abel, fighting won't make things better. My father's death had affected her the most. I can't imagine her pain. I picked up the phone and dialed my home number. Nothing. Finally, Abel answered after trying two more times. He didn't know it was me, so I hung up the phone. I couldn't speak to him. His voice would've made me even more frustrated. Then, something came to mind. Abel lives on campus. Why is he still at home? How many grievance days does the school allow? He's probably doing his work online. I put everything to the side. I'll visit later to check on her. I can drop my beef with Abel because I know she'll need my support. After searching every job site and filling out multiple online applications, I decided it was time to visit my mother. Kim was sleeping, so I left her that way. I drove to my house. Thankfully, I didn't wreak the car. I shut the motor off and walked to the door. I tried my key and the door didn't unlock. What the hell? I looked at the key, confused. It was the right one. I tried again and got the same results. Damn. My mother had to be pissed off if she changed the locks that fast. I knocked on the door for a long time. I knew she was home. Her car is parked in the driveway. Finally, Abel came to the door. Right, just the person I want to see. He was blocking my path into the house. He should know better than that, so I pushed by him. I called my mother's name. I went directly to her bedroom and opened the door. She wasn't in the room. Damn, did I miss her? She could've taken the other car. My mother never leaves the house. She stays at home most of the day. Abel might have gotten on her nerves, and she needed to clear her head. I heard Abel shouting my name from the bottom of the stairs. I paid him no mind. His chances of getting an ass whooping were high now I know he was alone. I went back down the stairs, passing Abel heading out to the backyard. She could be starting the garden she always talked about. I called her name, nothing. I came back in and Abel met me in the kitchen. I noticed he had the phone in his hand. He told me to leave the house. That wasn't going to happen. I live here, or did he forget? We got into a small argument before I asked where our mother was. He acted like it was a secret. It's our mother, why was he making it a big deal? What he said next was shocking. My mother broke down from anxiety, and he put her in a recovery home. I didn't believe one word. My mother is a strong-minded person. I demanded the truth and got the same answer. He smiled, and it triggered something on the inside. I came at him and he swiftly held up a piece of paper. I snatched the sheet from his hand. What? My brother had filed a restraining order.

Chapter 26
HILL HEIGHTS

I got back to the car. My blood was boiling, I'm on fire, hot. My mother was in a mental hospital. My brother got a fucking restraining order on me. I need to calm down and find a place called Hill Heights. That's where my mother is receiving treatment. I called Kim to let her know what was going on. She was fine with me having the car, no rush. I can take my time because she doesn't have to work today. Damn, I'm starting to feel like getting arrested was the worst thing to ever happen in my life, ever since things have gone downhill. My brother is evil, I went to jail, father murdered, no job, and my mother is in a hospital. What did the fuck happen to my life? I can't name one positive thing besides not dying a virgin. All I want is a damn job. Fuck! I had to air out my frustration. My life is a disaster. I sat in the car, thinking about how to solve my problems. I still haven't checked out my father's office. Ok, think. I came up with a plan. It's time to start getting stuff done. I started up the car. The first thing I need to do is visit Hill Heights. I pulled away, looking back at the house where I was raised, wondering if I'll ever come back, all of the memories. It broke my heart. It took thirty minutes to get to Hill Heights. I saw a sign that read, Hill Heights Mental Health Hospital. The front gate automatically opened, and I drove down a very long driveway. The road came to a roundabout. The place resembled a castle. I entered through tall double doors and walked directly to the front counter. The lady sitting there didn't recognize me standing in front of her. I noticed a small bell. I dinged the hell out of it, trying to wake her ass up. I felt disrespected. She had a crazy look on her face. She took the bell and slid it under the table. I don't care if she's upset. Nothing is nice about her appearance. She looks like a mean grandmother you didn't want to visit. She pointed to the pad that was on the opposite side of the bell. I looked at it and thought, we could've avoided that confrontation if it had been next to the bell. It was a registration sheet. Damn, something told me I had to wait. Hopefully, this lady works faster than the DMV. I filled it out and sat down in the lobby. I watched some crazy stuff happen while I waited. A woman was pacing back and forth in the hallway. I heard her mumbling something about meeting her husband. She looked no older than forty. I watched another woman standing in front of a TV, turned it on and off repeatedly. She kept shouting about her favorite TV show. It was coming on, and she couldn't find the channel. I saw an older man in the wheelchair reading a TV weekly. The magazine was upside down. I had to smile because he was telling the woman at the different television channels her show was on. I just shook my head. The lady at the counter finally called my name. I hopped up in a hurry to see my mother. She gave me directions to where she was having some free time. The hallway was something out of a movie. Patients were in the hall just standing around like zombies. Every person I walked by had a problem. Some people really need treatment. I was in a different world. The patients outside having free time were acting normal, unattended by a nurse. They couldn't climb over the gate anyway. It's tall with spikes. I found my mother. She was sitting in a chair by herself next to a rose bush. I walked over to her. I tried to figure out what to say. She had a vacant stare in her eyes. Why is she here? My mother doesn't belong in a place like this. She needs to be at home. I got a chair and sat across from her. I watched how she kept her eyes on the bush. The roses were beautiful. There were many different flowers, but it was the only rose bush in the yard. Suddenly, a tear fell from her cheek. I leaned in and hugged her. I called her mother and she didn't respond. Her face was emotionless. The roses had her attention, I said her name a second time and didn't get an answer. She never looked away from the bush. My feelings were hurt. My mother had a mental breakdown after my father died. I got teary eyed just thinking about him. Even though she didn't respond, I kept talking. I will remind her of the amazing life we share and how she has a wonderful son. In the end, I will be there for her. That's how my father raised me. We will make it through this together. That's what I believe, and nothing will change my mind.

Chapter 27

ME AND MY GIRLFRIEND

I made it back to the apartment. Kim was in the kitchen cooking and smoking a blunt. I threw the keys on the dining room table and sat in the living room. I was frustrated. There were a lot of things on my mind. Kim noticed the look on my face. She became worried because she stopped what she was doing and sat next to me. I leaned back on the sofa. I just need a break. I knew Kim wanted to talk, but she didn't say anything, she understood me. She put her hand on my thigh and caressed it, her hand was warm and soft. She leaned back and put her head on my shoulder. She knew what I was going through. I'm not going to pretend to be happy. What happened to my mother broke me. Somehow, I knew Kim could fix me. We were created for each other. I felt in my heart that she was the one for me. Her energy made me feel better. That's what I need to get through this situation. It's the same connection my father had with my mother. I exhaled, ready to speak. I went over everything that happened. I mainly spoke about my mother. I explained to her that my mom didn't even recognize me. It was hard to talk about. She helped keep my emotions in check. I hated the fact Abel put her in a hospital. I thought he loved her. I would've never done that to my mother. If I had money to take care of her, it wouldn't be this bad. I could bring her home. I took the blunt from her mouth. I remember how it made me feel. Drugs won't help deal with my emotions, although smoking weed made me feel relaxed. Bad shit is following me around, and I need a way to shake these demons. If I relax my mind, I can focus on the future. I hit the blunt, thinking about my next move. I'm not about to fold under pressure. My father taught me how to survive. I watched him deal with pressure for his entire life. I lived at his office. He knew how to rise from under difficult circumstances, exactly what I'll do by any means. I need some money, and I couldn't count on a job. It's like finding a one-hundred-dollar bill. You have a slim chance, but it could happen. I have a murder hanging over my head. Many people liked her, it was all over the news. Kim got up and checked the jerk chicken in the oven. Smoking gave me a different desire, food. That was the only thing on my mind after the smell hit me from the kitchen. Damn, it wasn't ready. I turned on the TV and scanned through the channels. I wasn't in the mood to watch TV, but something in my head kept saying grab the remote control. That could have been me just being high. I flipped through a few channels. I felt like the lady at the hospital. I was looking for something but didn't know what I was trying to find. I heard the old guy in the back of my mind. Finally, I stopped on the Channel Five News. Maybe there will be breaking news about the investigation of my father's death. I'm wondering if they're trying hard to solve the case. My father is from another country. Things don't get done as fast. None of the news reports were of interest. The sports update was the best part of the show until breaking news flashed on the screen. BREAKING NEWS: Three-Armed Bank Robbers Escape with $70,000. Damn, I could use seventy grand. The police had no leads on the suspects. The robbers got away clean. Footage was shown of the robbers committing the crime. Three men ran into the bank wearing masks with guns. One suspect held a security guard at gunpoint with a shotgun. The second guy was fast on his feet. He hopped over the counter with a bag in his hand. I knew he was going after the money. The third guy intrigued me the most. He paced back and forth, standing on the counter, fearlessly aiming an assault rifle at anyone who moved. He's the leader. They hurried from the scene, gone. It took them less than two minutes, a quick job. I wasn't going to make that much money for a long time. I sat up on the sofa. I was caught by surprise when I noticed Kim standing over me. She was paying very close attention to the report. I'll never forget what she said next. "We could've robbed that bank."

Chapter 28

THE ROUND-UP

I turned off the TV. I faced Kim with a serious look on my face. It was more serious than I had ever looked. The next words came spilling out of my mouth. My mind took control of my lips. "You want to?" I looked her dead in the eyes when I spoke. I didn't even crack a smile. I could tell she knew how serious I was about the question. "You want to rob a bank, really?" She countered. I didn't have to think about an answer. I want to do this without a doubt. "Yes, I'm serious. You saw those fools on TV escape with $70,000. That's a lot of money in a short period. We can do it in less time. I know we can. That could've been us with all that money." "You think we could've gotten away from the police?" She asked in a concerning interest. I had her attention and could tell by her body language. She was interested. I wasn't just talking to myself. "Yes, baby. You and I, together. We're smarter and faster than those guys. All we need are masks and guns." "I don't want to kill innocent people." She took the blunt and sat down next to me. "You won't have to kill anyone. The robbers didn't have to fire their weapons. Everything was fine for them. Why wouldn't it be the same for us?" I asked. I believed what I was saying, and that's how I want her to perceive my message. I stood up from the sofa, convinced we could rob a bank. "You're right," She answered softly. "But those guys were professionals. They probably robbed banks for a living." That could be true, damn good point. They could be professionals. The robbery did seem orchestrated. I'm swimming in uncharted waters. We had to have a well thought out plan. We need to be fully aware of the situation, or something drastic could happen. One of us could get killed. That would be a devastating outcome. I took a few seconds to gather my thoughts, thinking about my situation. "I'm sure at one point those guys were in the same position we're in now, trying to figure out if it was the right move for them to make, wondering if they could pull it off, and contemplating if one of them would get killed. You know what they did?" I saw her slowly shake her head no. "They went with their instincts. A gut feeling that told them to do so, telling them they would be successful. I promise if you're with me, I'll do everything in my power to make sure you're ok. I need your help to come up with a great plan. That's the key. Not just instincts and actions. I know thirty percent is me being emotional, but I know we're smart enough to make this work." I looked at her out of love. I won't do this without her. She's all I have left, and I'll never act out of pocket. What we have together is hard to find. Our relationship is the most important thing in the world. "What's the plan?" She asked. I was shocked. She said yes. That was unexpected. I thought we were both high, and I would be back looking for a job tomorrow. That wasn't the case. I'm more confident than high. "First, we need to get a team. People we can sure as hell trust." I assured her. "We need lookouts and a driver. I have a few people in mind."

Chapter 29
CLOSE FRIENDS

I knew three people who could be trustworthy. If anybody would have my back, it'll be my boys. They might think I'm insane, but who gives a damn. I'm at the end. This was asking a lot as if there isn't another way to make money. I only hope we can still be friends if they don't accept my offer. After gathering my thoughts on what I was going to say, I called Smoke. We spoke the other day. He should be back in town. The phone rang a few times before he answered. "What's good, Kane?" He answered the phone in a low tone. "I'm cool, is everything alright with you?" I asked. "You sound sick." I didn't want to come straight out with, let's rob a fucking bank, homeboy. "I'm hurting right now," He said emotionally. "Trying to figure out how to help my grandma." Damn, that's right. I forget that his grandma was sick. I can't ask him to rob a bank. That would be wrong on my part as a friend. "I'm sorry to hear that, I hope she gets better." "I don't know," He said with a soft voice. "She needs a $30,000 heart surgery and I don't have that kind of bread." Smoke's grandma needs $30,000 for heart surgery? "Insurance won't cover the payment?" I asked with concern. Smoke is real close to his grandma. She had taken care of him for his entire life. His parents were crack addicts. They died when he was eight years old. They're originally from South Carolina. That's where his grandma is being cared for by her daughter. Smoke has been living with his uncle ever since. "They do," He told me. "Only a percentage. The heart surgery cost a hundred thousand dollars. They will only pay seventy percent, leaving me with the other thirty percent to pay up-front." "Damn," I was lost for words for a moment. "There's no one else in your family that can help come up with the money?" "No," He sounded upset about it. "Everybody got bills to pay. It's crazy. My grandma took care of everybody in our family. If it weren't for her daughter, I would be the only person trying to help." I thought about not asking Smoke to help with the bank job. I slowly changed my mind. He needs the money more than me. If everything goes to plan, this could help with his situation. "Smoke, I'm going to be real with you. I might be able to help you get the money. I don't want to talk about it over the phone. What I need for you to do is meet me at Kim's apartment. It's off Pleasant Hill Road in Duluth." He agreed, and I gave him the directions. My next phone call went to Redd. I think we're close enough friends where I could trust him. Especially after he gave me the heads up to run from the cops. Redd picked up the phone, sounding dead tired. "Kane," He said sleepily. "What's good, playa?" "Nothing much," I said. "Just checking on you." How's your leg? I'm sure you'll be jumping through the roof once it heals." I wanted to make some type of conversation before asking him to come over. "My man," He had a skeptical tone of voice. "You'll never believe what I have to tell you." "What's up?" I asked. I felt that he was about to drop some bad news. "The doctor said I would never be able to run or jump like before the injury. I fucked up some vital ligaments in my leg. I'll never be able to play ball the same. It's over for me. My scholarships are gone. I'll never be able to play college ball, let alone make the league. Kane, I don't know what to do with myself." I felt bad for Redd. Having a dream taken away from you hurts. My dream was taken away when I got arrested. I know where he's coming from, it's a dark place intended to keep you depressed. "Don't worry. I can help. Can you come to Kim's apartment in Duluth? I want to speak with you face to face, and I need a favor?" "Yes," He assured me. "What's the favor?" "I need you to call Bear and tell him to slide through. I have to speak to him, as well." "No problem." I ended the call. I have my team. Now... convince them to rob a bank.

Chapter 30

LIFE INSURANCE

I sat on the couch, waiting for my friends. Kim was in the bathroom, taking a shower. I went into the bedroom. The room smelt like Bath & Body products. I found a pen and a piece of paper. It was time to work on an outline. I sat down at the dining room table and thought about what to say. The most important thing is not to sound stupid. They have to know I'm in the right state of mind and not crazy. The first thing they'll want to know is why I want to rob a bank. That's an easy question, money. I wrote down several other questions and answers. My reason for doing this had to be meaningful. My back is against the wall, and nobody wants to hire me. I won't depend on Kim for money. She shouldn't have to take care of a grown man. My father was murdered, and I don't have the money to hire a private investigator. My mother needs support and that is an issue. The only way I can fix any of my problems is money. When I finished the first part of the outline. I went over everything in my head, preparing my speech. The doorbell rang and I got up to answer it. "Smoke." I gave him some dap when he walked through the door. "I'm glad you made it." "Kane," He sounded cool. "What's good, fam? I know my little sis been on your head about finding a job since you got out. Where she at?" Smoke appeared to be fine, but he couldn't hide his emotions from me. He's hurt because I know how much he loves his grandma. "She's in the bedroom." I told him. She'll be out here to meet us in a few minutes." "Alright," He took a seat on the sofa. "So how are you able to help with my situation? I don't want any handouts. I know your family is wealthy. You know I'll work for mines." Smoke's family doesn't have money like my family. His grandma worked hard for her entire life. She paid for his enrollment in private school. He had to drop out and get a GED after she got sick. I don't have control of our family's income, and he's about to find that out. He's still unaware of my father's death and my mother's mental health. "I'll explain everything once the others arrive and I know you're not looking for any handouts. Trust me. You have more money than me. I'm broke as a joke." I want him to feel comfortable before I explain myself. "I feel you," He said. "Being locked up for that long will have you fucked up on the streets. It's damn near impossible to recover without the proper support. You'll be just fine." He looked a bit more relaxed. "Who are we waiting for?" There was a knock at the door. That happened right on time. "They're here." I walked over to the door to let in Redd and Bear. "What's good?" I gave them dap as they walked through the door. "I'm good," Redd said. "Feeling like a normal person now that I can walk on my own." "Tired," Bear spoke up. "I don't get any sleep with my mother nagging all the time. All she talks about is getting a job with my lazy ass. She's driving me crazy, dawg." Smoke stood and greeted them both in the living room. I have everyone together. Kim came from the bedroom and said hello to the crew. After we got settled, she offered drinks. While she was handling that, I walked in front of the TV to get their attention. It was time to let them know what I had planned. "I appreciate you all for coming. What I have to say might change your lives forever if you decide to take my offer. There is a chance you all can make some serious money. If any of you decide not to accept, forget about everything you heard here today." I had their attention. "I think all of us could use a break. Money is an issue for every single person in this room. Do you feel like no matter how hard you try shit isn't working in your favor? I'm dealing with the same type of stressful situations, and my family has money. Times are rough for everyone. Smoke, you need money for your grandma's surgery. Redd, what did your doctor say? Bear, you have a sleeping disorder. You could've played in the NFL. We're million-dollar guys settling for less. Our futures were bright. Now we're nobodies, struggling to make ends meet." "You told us our problems," Smoke spoke up. "But what about you? It sounds good, but what's the catch? I'm not selling drugs. Your two years were good enough for me." "My father was murdered." I dropped the news, and they all had shocked facial expressions. "He was killed the day I was released from jail. The police are still looking for the suspect. It caused my mother to have a mental breakdown. She's staying at a hospital called Hill Heights. She won't speak to anybody. When I went to visit, she didn't speak to me, and I'm her son. It hurts because I should've been closer to her. Everything we own is in her name. I don't have the money to care for her, and no one will give me a job. Now you know my problems." Smoke shook his head. "Damn, I'm sorry to hear that. "Fuck," I heard Redd mutter. "You good?" "Sorry for your loss," Bear said. "He was a cool dude and I love your mom." "Thanks," I told them. "I appreciate your concern. Everything will be fine. Kim is helping me get through this and with your help. Things could get better." "So, what do you have in mind?" Smoke asked. I made sure they all were looking directly in my eyes. "Let's rob a fucking bank."

Chapter 31
SITUATIONS "ROB A BANK!"

Smoke jumped out of his seat hysterically. "Man, have you lost your damn mind?" The look on his face was very serious. "OK," Redd said sarcastically. "Let's all go to prison. The part about your parents was emotional, but this is a drastic turn of conversation." "No," Kim answered while setting drinks on the table. "He didn't lose his mind. I think we can do it if we're smart about how we approach the situation." I looked across the room to see how they would respond after Kim spoke. The only person out of the bunch who didn't think I was crazy was Bear. That's because he's asleep. I stayed quiet for a moment. "Oh, shit." Smoke said. "Sis, don't tell me he got you convinced this is cool?" "Yeah, he got her." Redd spoke up. "I can see it in her eyes. They're both crazy." "We're not crazy." She defended me. "I just think he has a good point. Think about what he's trying to tell you. Redd, your leg is shot. You'll never play basketball the same. You were a star. Now you'll end up working a nine to five in a fast food place. And Smoke, your grandmother needs heart surgery. You have a thirty-thousand-dollar problem that can't wait, right? Who wants to lend you the money? She could die, and I know you don't want that to happen. You need this more than anyone. I've been friends with you longer than anybody here. I know your grandmother. You and I are like brother and sister. I don't want her to die. And look at Bear. He's asleep. Who wants to hire a guy who sleeps all day? We're not trying to become career bank robbers. This is a once in a lifetime deal that could potentially fix all of our problems." Damn, Kim had my back one hundred percent. She made me feel good about the situation. She's my queen. I watched how everyone began to act differently. Smoke was looking down at his hands. I know he felt in his heart what Kim had said. His grandma could die. Redd was massaging the scar on his leg, probably thinking she's right. That's what I got from the look on his face. Bear's asleep, I'll convince him later. I don't know how to feel at this point. I might have lost two close friends. I kept searching my mind for something to say. Suddenly, Redd broke the silence in the room. "Fuck," Redd muttered emotionally. "She's a hell of a motivational speaker. Kane, you better not get me killed. I'm down." "Damn," Smoke spoke quietly. "I can't believe I'm about to say this, but… I'm down. I need this bread. My grandma's life depends on money. What the fuck." What I heard from their mouths was unbelievable. They just put their lives in my hands. They're willing to die for a chance to fix their problems. I feel the same way as them. "Ok, cool. We're all down, so we can move forward with the plan." "What about Bear?" Redd asked "Right," I sighed. He was sleeping. "Let's wake him up and find out." It was hard waking Bear up, but he finally opened his eyes. "Bear!" I yelled in his ear. His eyes were red when he looked at me. "You want to rob a bank?" I got straight to the point. "Sure," He began smiling. "I need a gun and I want to be the getaway driver like in the movies." I looked at Bear like he planned to rob a bank all along. "Ok, that's cool with me. Does anybody else have a problem with Bear being the getaway driver?" "I'm cool with it." Smoke said. "If you're cool with it." Redd spoke up. "I don't have a problem." "Hold on for a second." Kim interrupted. "Are you sure this is the right decision? Bear has a sleeping disorder. He'll be asleep by the time we get back to the vehicle. That's a problem we don't want waiting for us." Damn, Kim had a good point. Bear sleeps like a grizzly in the winter. We can't afford something like that to happen. "I won't fall asleep." Bear interrupted my thoughts. "How do we know that?" Kim asked curiously. "I only fall asleep when I'm not busy." He elaborated. "While I'm waiting, I could pretend the vehicle broke down, lift the hood, and act like I'm waiting for a tow truck. I'll provide surveillance. You'll need a lookout on the outside. I won't let you all down. Please, let me be the driver?" We all agreed, even though It wasn't a good idea. Bear is big and slow. He'll only hold us up on the inside. So, we all concluded the best thing for him to do is drive. Now we need a full proof masterplan.

Chapter 32
WEST WOOD BANK

We came up with a plan in four days. We decided to hit West Wood Bank. We left Kim's apartment in two vehicles. I rode with Kim in her car. Smoke drove Redd and Bear in his car. Our main goal was not to be seen together. That would be suspicious. Kim and I would go inside and ask about opening a bank account. Redd already had an account there, and Smoke would tag along. They'll dress like a college fraternity. Bear is off for the day. It shouldn't be that hard watching out for the police. Every part of the plan is vital. We parked at the bank. I surveyed the scenery. People moved around open minded. Who would've thought someone was here to case the bank? There were different kinds of people in the area. A few brought their kids. Some were probably on a lunch break. I've never looked at a place like this before. We're going to walk in there and act normal. We got out of the car and walked to the front door while holding hands. We looked like the perfect couple. We are the perfect couple. I opened the door for her. The inside of the bank was active. I counted about seven bank tellers and roughly twenty people waiting in line. An older woman was working in a side office. She's more than likely the bank manager. I was very careful, trying not to be noticeable. We stood in a line waiting for our turn. Two people were ahead of us. A man wearing a suit stood directly in front of us. He was holding a briefcase. If I had to guess, I would say he's here to make a deposit. A pregnant woman stood in front of him. She looked around seven months and ready to pop. I continue to survey the bank. I found a clock on the back wall, 1:20 pm. We've been inside for two minutes. Smoke and Redd should walk through the front door any second. A security guard was positioned outside the vault. It was wide open. Damn, that easy? I used my peripheral vision to inspect the vault. The money was right in front of me. The guard didn't look tough. He was a shrimp. I'm bigger and stronger. I spotted a gun on his waist. I wonder if he ever had to shoot somebody? We moved up one space in line. I wanted to point out the vault to Kim without being obvious. I signed to her in the direction of the guard. She kind of nodded her head discreetly. The man in the suit approached the next available teller. We were next in line. I checked my watch and it was 1:22 pm. I played it cool while watching the front door. Smoke and Redd had walked through on time. A couple waited behind us in line. They were bickering at each other. I held Kim's chin and told her I love her. I made sure people around us could hear, including the tellers. I kissed her on the lips. We were trying to appear to be two love birds in a bank. A small precaution to stay off the radar. We were up next. The teller was a woman, good. I let Kim do all the talking. She was better at conversing than me. She opened a new checking account and deposited one hundred dollars. We thanked the woman and I took a brochure off the counter. We passed Smoke and Redd coolly without speaking a word. Everything was moving according to the plan.

Chapter 33
THE DREAD HEAD PLAN

We drove past the bank every day at 1:20 pm for three straight days. The exact time the vault was open. Redd, Smoke, and I would drive by the bank on separate days. I switched it up to stay low-key. That's something my father told me. Keep your opponent guessing and don't get caught off guard. Even bad guys use their brains. I'm not rushing in this situation bull headed. It was time to follow through with the plan. Bear got someone to rent a van. We'll get out across the street, and then he'll wait for us around the corner. Redd will guard the main entrance. Nobody can enter or leave once we're inside of the bank. Kim will wear a wig and be there ahead of time. Hopefully, she'll be able to spot any undercover officers. Smoke's job will require speed. He has two minutes to grab as much money as he can from inside the vault. I'll disarm the guard and then watch for any possible threats. We have black masks and handguns. Bear didn't need a mask but argued about getting one. He thought they made you look cool. I gave him one, but not before I reasoned with him. I told him that he couldn't wear it during the robbery. A big guy walking around in a hockey mask will set off an alarm. We have a change of clothes in the van. Redd got us three 9mm handguns from his father's gun collection. That's more than enough firepower. We parked Kim's Lexus in a grocery store parking lot. It will be our escape vehicle. Smoke and Redd will walk to a restaurant in the area. Redd will call beforehand to place an order. Bear will dump the van behind a grocery store where Smoke parked his car. We check the area thoroughly for cameras, and there were none. After dumping the van, he'll set it on fire. Then enter the store and grab a few things to create an alibi. The next day, we will meet at Kim's apartment. It'll be the safest place to divide the money. Everyone met at the apartment to go over the plan a final time. We have to be fully prepared in case something goes wrong. I made sure each person knew their job. Any mistake will make us vulnerable. They were ready. We broke from the apartment like a football squad. Kim dropped us off at the van before taking the car to the grocery store. She'll have to walk two blocks before reaching the bank. Redd went to a nearby payphone and ordered the food using a fake name. Time to work. We loaded in the van, and Bear pulled off toward the bank. We got dressed in all black clothes on the way. We arrived just before Kim walked inside. I looked down at my watch, ten minutes before start time. I took a deep breath. My hands started shaking because I was nervous. I've never done anything this criminal. My life was about to change. I held the 9mm firm in my hand. I gripped the handle thinking, what if I have to put in work? I answered that question by placing the mask over my face. My dreads hung loosely, covering my neck. I looked toward the back of the van. We all looked like a group of savages from the movie Predator. After two minutes of being paranoid, I emerged from the vehicle. Surprisingly, my crew followed. We ran from across the street into the bank.

Chapter 34
PREDATORS

"Everybody lay the fuck down!" I yelled while storming into the bank. People were panicking and hurrying down on the floor. I flashed the nine in every direction and saw a look of concern on their faces. I'm actually robbing a bank. It was unbelievable. Something in my head told me to leave. And something else told me to get that fucking paper. You need this money for your family. Your father is not here to save you. Your mother needs support. Smoke is depending on this money for his grandma's heart surgery. You sold Redd and Bear a dream. I'm carrying this shit out and that's final. I'm their leader. I can't back out now. Tell me what you think of us? We're a bunch of no good, dread headed, savage beast, that will do anything for money. That's how you feel? Right now, I'm at the point where you're right. This is what life has turned us into, predators. I searched for the officer who should be standing by the vault. It was open and the guard stood in the same spot. I aimed in his direction and fired. Intentionally, missing on purpose, trying not to hit him. It was a warning shot, letting him know I wasn't bullshitting, get the fuck down. The guard tried to close the vault after he heard trouble. Smoke was too fast for the old man. He hurdled over the counter with lightning speed and caught the vault door in mid-swing. I followed behind and gun butt the guard in the back of his head. "Get down!" It was a violent hit causing him to fall to the floor, out cold. I disarmed him. Smoke turned back around. "Get the money," I told him. I propped the officer against the door to keep it from closing on Smoke, locking him inside. That wouldn't be good. I hopped on the counter and walked down the line of tellers. I checked my watch. "One minute!" I yelled, keeping everybody on task. I checked the front door and Redd stood guard like a dog. I searched the floor of hostages for Kim. I saw her positioned between two women. She looked up at me. I caught her eyes, signaling to the woman on her left. The woman was making a move. She slowly eased her hand behind her back. I leaped off the counter and hurried over before things got worse. I pressed the gun to the back of her head and she froze. "God forbid that I have to blow your fucking brains all over the floor. They'll be mopping your shit up later." I spoke harshly. It sounded good, but I'm not killing anybody. I wanted to scare her into believing what I said. I patted her down and found a gun on her back waist and a badge. She works for the Atlanta Police Department. Possibly an off-duty officer or undercover. Either way, she's in the thick of things. I holstered her gun on the back of my waist. I stood and tossed the officer's badge on her back. I took Kim hostage and placed the gun to her head. "Anybody tries something stupid. This woman is dead!" She screamed and pretended to fight me off. When I felt all eyes on me, I forced her down on her knees while still holding the gun to her head. She started crying, making her part feel believable. She won't have to answer any questions when the cops arrive. We didn't want any contact with the law. I checked my watch. "Twenty seconds!" I yelled. Everything was going smoothly. I signaled for Redd to unlock the door. I watched him check the front entrance. He yelled back to me. "Clear!" I checked the time on my watch. "Let's move!" I yelled. I backed away while holding the gun to Kim's head, taking her hostage. Smoke sprinted from the vault and over the counter. It was amazing how full the bag looked. He left out of the bank first. Redd was the last to leave. When I got a reasonable distance from the door, I released Kim and we made our getaway.

Chapter 35
PROBLEMS SOLVED

I heard police sirens as we ran from the bank. We made it around the corner where Bear was waiting in the van. The sirens got louder as they got closer. It didn't matter, though. We were gone. Two things in this world you can't take back. Bullets in a gun and words out your mouth. It was something my father told me. He was wrong. I can't take back what I just did if we get caught. We got the money. I saw Smoke in front, flying with the bag in his hand. He got in the van and slid the side door open for us to enter. I thought I would never make it. It felt like an eternity. I helped Kim get in first and then Redd. I slid the door shut and rotated to the passenger seat. I told Bear to get us the hell out of there, and he didn't respond. What? I noticed he put the mask on. He sat there stiff with his head back on the seat rest. His large hands were on the steering wheel at a 10 to 2 like he was ready to pull off. I yelled in his ear, nothing.

He was alive because his enormous chest heaved breaths of air. I listened to everyone in the back shout, get us the fuck out of here! Especially Kim. What the fuck is Bear's problem? Is he trying to get us caught? I slid his mask to the top of his forehead. Damn, I knew it. He fell asleep with the mask over his face. The van was idling, I heard the engine running. Bear was a problem. I have to think fast. We don't have ten minutes to wake him. In another two minutes, the police will be all over the bank. Thirty seconds from that point, they'll find us trying to wake him like some damn fools. Why didn't I listen to Kim in the first place? I had a feeling she was right. Think, think, think. I came up with the only thing I could do out of fear of going to jail. A cot was waiting for us all in prison if this doesn't work. I cocked my hand back to Jamaica. Bear will have to forgive me. Peoples' lives were at stake. I closed my fist, ready to knock his lights out, or should I say, turn them on. Suddenly, I was caught by surprise. A loud, ringing sound erupted. What the hell was that? I looked down where the sound was coming from, and I saw a small white device with a timer on it rested in his lap. My eyes moved from the timer to his eyes. It woke him up. Hell, yeah! "Bear, get us the hell out of here!" He saw the panic look on my face and sped off. The van shot from the back alley onto the street. I heard the tires squeal on the pavement. I told him to slow down. We don't want to look suspicious. Ten seconds of driving and the police shot passed us. They were speeding, coming from the opposite direction. Oh, shit. I thought for sure one of the cop cars would stop in front of us. I felt they knew we robbed the bank. A feeling of uncertainty crept up on me. The ops were close, and I was trying to maintain my composure. I checked the rearview as we gained some distance. They surrounded the bank with guns. I watched them enter. I smiled as we turned the corner, making a clean getaway. Myself conscious settled, knowing we were at a safe distance. We got to the grocery store and began the next phase. Everyone changed clothes except m, so I hurried to the back and stripped down. I put on a pair of casual clothes and tied my hair. Smoke and Redd were already on their way to the restaurant. I grabbed the bag of money. It was heavy. I tossed it in the trunk and got in the car. Problems solved.

Chapter 36
DREAD HEAD BANK ROBBERS

Kim and I made it back to her apartment safely. The first thing I did was put the bag in the closet, and then I grabbed my cell phone. I had to check on my friends. I want to make sure they're okay. I sat down on the living room couch. Kim sat on the sofa across from me. She grabbed the remote control off the table and turned on the TV. The first person I called was Smoke. The phone rang and a few times before he answered. "What's good, man?" I felt relieved he picked up the line. "Y'all straight?" "We're good," He assured me. "We're picking up some food, big dawg. I left my phone in the car. What's up with you and her?" I knew he wasn't asking about Kim. He wanted to know the bag was safe? "Everything is good with her. No worries." I answered, letting him know the bag was secured. "Ok," He said. "I'll slide through tomorrow and hangout." "Cool," I said. "Whenever you're ready." "Bet,

I'll let Redd know." He hung up the phone. I was about to call Bear. He had a tough job to finish, burn the vehicle, and duck off unnoticed. I looked at Kim, and she focused on the TV. My attention went from her to the TV. Oh, shit. The news was covering the bank robbery. I held the phone in my hand, unable to dial Bear's number. I was captivated by the report. Cops were everywhere on the scene. The cameraman followed a woman reporter around the bank. The reporter began interviewing people who witnessed the robbery. A man said, ten guys ran into the bank, and five of them held him down. That's why he couldn't save the day. I smiled at his exaggeration. The reporter interviewed a woman next. She told the newswoman three men who resembled lions held her hostage. They looked savage and one grabbed her breasts. He violated her in every way and offered sex. That's crazy. She lost her mind. What the hell was she talking about? Violated her? Please, not in a million years with that face. The last person she interviewed was the woman cop I disarmed. She said three men wearing black masks entered the bank. They were very professional and took precise orders from their leader. They used handguns to hold everyone hostage. The guy calling the shots disarmed her of her weapon. She pointed out the men wore their hair in a particular fashion, dreadlocks. She said everything they did was well planned. They didn't hesitate and were swift on their feet. Before the interview was over, she described a woman they had taken hostage. The Chief of police had the floor. He said if anyone has information that could lead to an arrest, please call the police. They can forget about seeing us again because that was the last time. I don't plan to make a living, robbing banks. Kim kept watching the news. I called Bear to make sure he was safe. His phone rang and I got his voicemail. I tried two more times. Damn, I don't want to panic. Stay calm. I was desperate to know if he was alright. I dialed his home phone number, and his mother answered. I asked her nicely if her son was home. She told me to hold on while she checked. I held on the line praying, she'll put him on the phone. She got back on the line and told me he was asleep. She complained about Bear playing hockey all day. And added, his no job having, excuse for a son, fell asleep with the damn mask on.

Chapter 37
THREE INDIANS -JORDAN-

It's been two and a half weeks, and I didn't gain any ground on the Simmons case. His office was officially closed. Not one of his former employees were potential suspects. They talked about how good of a family man he was and provided nothing about his personal life. I found out Jar used to bring Kane to work when he was younger. They all saw Kane as a little brother. Noti and Able Simmons barely visited the office. I learned nothing new about them. No one thought Jar was tied to any criminal activity. To them, he was the best boss in the world. I was amazed by how much praise Jar received from his workers. I began to feel like he was the best boss ever. Why wouldn't he be? I wish my boss were that amazing to work for. Jar was the best thing since sliced bread. He seemed too good to be true. How many men were built for fatherhood like Jar? Not that many, I assume. Somebody needs to hand this guy the Man of the Year award. I didn't get any information from his family. What surprised me the most was his wife having a mental breakdown. I went by their home last week, and that evil kid Abel answered the door. Man, it's something about the way that kid looked at me. He scared me to death. I asked him was now a good time to speak to his mother. He stared back at me with the coldest eyes I've ever seen in my life. I felt a chill roll down my spine. I wanted to forget about the question. I felt like turning around and walking far away. My legs were weak and I lost my breath. He looked at me, confused. He offered something to drink and said I could rest inside. Hell no. I wasn't about to go in there alone with him. I didn't even like being around the kid. I was suffocating on my own breath. I don't know how I got the words out, but I asked him a second time to speak with his mother. He shrugged his shoulders and said it depends on how you're planning for her to answer. I'm not the one for playing mind games, and I don't beat around the bush. I asked what he meant. He smirked and looked deep in my eyes. I felt pressured and it caused me to look away. I would rather be around mafia guys than Abel. After a moment of silence, he said. "Hill Heights." "Hill Heights," I muttered to myself. What is Hill Heights? I didn't get a chance to talk to his mother. He put her in a mental health hospital. Her husband was dead, and it caused her to have a mental breakdown. That was all I needed to know.

I didn't want to be around Abel any longer. If I need any more questions answered, Rick could handle it. He knew how to keep his composure when speaking to this kid. I hurried back to my car. His eyes followed me the entire way because I felt them staring at me. It was a relief to be a safe distance from the kid. I leaned back in my seat and thought about their mother's sudden breakdown. I put the key in the ignition and started the car, and something told me to look to the side. I saw Abel breathing on my passenger window. I yelped like a 5-year-old. I thought he wanted to harm me. That was the final straw. I put my hand on my weapon, ready to put a bullet in him for no reason. I watched his eyes dropped down to where my hand rested. He slowly backed off the window, apparently trying to tell me something. Man, my nerves were bad. My hands shook like a drug addict. I rolled the window down halfway, just enough to hear what the evil genius had to say. Surprisingly, he asked if needed directions to the mental hospital. I did. He gave me the address and I saved it in my GPS. I thanked him and sped off. He didn't need an opportunity to say bye. We're not friends. I got the hell out of there. Ever since that day, I haven't spoken to Abel. I've been at the office doing paperwork and trying to keep a close eye on Kane. Unfortunately, that's not working out too well. I watched the Simmons house for three days on a stakeout. I was hoping to see Kane. He must have slipped by somehow because he was a no show. He could be living with someone else, maybe staying with a friend or girlfriend. That's something I noted to look into. The kid gave me the slip. I closed my eyes and leaned back in my office chair. I was thinking about where Kane might have gone and why he wouldn't be living at home. I would love to live in a house like theirs. It's huge. Suddenly, I heard footsteps, and someone grabbed my shoulder. I almost fell out of my seat. My foot caught under the desk and allowed me to regain my balance. "What the hell," I growled while almost falling backwards. That would've been a bad way to start the day. It was Rick. He had a frantic look on his face. "What did I tell you about surprising people, Rick?" "Sorry," He said, exhausted. "Something big just came up. There's a bank robbery in progress." A bank robbery! That's what I'm talking about. I was ready to bust some bad guys. It's been dead around here all week. "Where?" I asked while grabbing my coat, badge, and gun. "At Westwood Bank." He replied. "Come on," I told him. "You can ride with me. I know exactly how to get there." Westwood Bank is where I opened my first savings account when I worked for the Atlanta police. We made a quick stop by the weapons department. A few members of the team were gearing up to get dirty. I grabbed a shotgun, helmet, and a Kevlar bulletproof vest. After getting what I needed to kick some ass, we took off in a hurry. We got in my Benz and sped out of the parking lot. I want to be the first agent on the scene. That's how I liked it. The first to shoot somebody or make the bust. I'm okay with either outcome. I maneuvered through traffic, making our way to the bank. I skid the car to a stop in front of the building. I swiftly got out of the vehicle, leaving my door open for cover. Rick copied my movement on his side. The Chief of police spoke in a megaphone. He told the suspects to come out with their hands up after a few seconds of not having a response. I was leaning toward taking a chance on entering the bank. A woman suddenly emerged from the bank holding up her hands. She was flashing a police badge. She informed us the robbers fled the scene. It went in one ear and out the other. I stormed inside and searched the bank anyway, looking for suspects. By the time I was finished, live news teams were outside reporting the crime. Damn, no action. The policewoman mentioned seeing only three male suspects. That's three Indians I had to hunt down. Game on.

Chapter 38
THE CALL

The Planner was back in the same position staring at the paintings. He was careful not to let anyone who walked past see his face. He discreetly checked the location of the security guards. They were stationed where he thought they would be. He looked up and saw the only revolving camera in the room. It rotated every five seconds, surveying the area. He counted down in his head and turned with the device so it wouldn't catch his face. He calculated every move to avoid suspicion. Something that never happened before caught his attention. One of the guards stepped away from the diamond. They were becoming lazy. Nobody would have enough courage to steal it. He thought today would be the day to make an attempt. He wanted the rock bad and not because of the overwhelming value. The attention it would bring was nearly more intriguing than swiping it. Private collectors would be paranoid, causing them to panic. A jewel thief on the loose in their city. Tuck away all of your valuable possessions if you want to keep them. He would be famous for the biggest heist in history. He stared at the diamond long enough. Two seconds before the camera would turn in his direction. He was gone from the museum forever. That would be his last time looking at the diamond through security glass. The precious stone would be in his hands the next time he saw it. He made it back to his vehicle, parked down the street from the building. The parking garage was off limits due to the number of cameras in the lot. He closed the door and sat there for a moment. He swiped a cell phone from a person in the museum. There couldn't be anything that led back to him. It was time to put his masterplan in action. He made sure the number came through as private. He used a voice changer for the phone. "Simmons residence," Abel answered the line. "Yes," The Planner said. "I'm well aware, Abel." "Who are you and why do you need a voice changer?" Abel said with an attitude. "I'm guessing you have bad intentions." "You're a smart boy." He said. "Let's not focus on my voice. I have an offer for you and if you choose to refuse. There's no need to worry who I am." "How did you get this number," Abel retorted. "And how do you know my name?" "Your father, Abel." The Planner assured him. "He was more than a businessman. It wasn't that hard gathering information on your family." Abel thought for a moment. He ran his mind back to the black notebook he stole from his father after murdering him. His father ran a secret business. Even his mother wasn't aware of it. The information inside the book was life threatening. If the details leaked to the law, his family wouldn't be able to recover. This situation wasn't any different. The person on the line could be working against him, but why use a voice changer? Abel thought about expanding his power. That was the main reason for killing his father and stealing the notebook. "What is your offer?" The Planner smiled. He had Abel right where he wanted him. "How does five million dollars sound?" That was a small fee from his payment for stealing the diamond. That's if he had to pay him. The plan was to kill Abel after he handed over the diamond. That's how he handled business, no witnesses, and no leads. "I'm listening," Abel spoke. "Five million is worth a brief conversation." The Planner gave Abel information about the diamond and the museum. He accepted the job. He told Abel the best time to make a move on the rock. Abel was activated. After he finished the call, he dialed a number to another worthy candidate.

Chapter 39
LIFE CHANGING -KANE-

I left Hill Heights mental health hospital. I decided to visit my mother and try to help with her progression. I needed somewhere to be seen after the bank robbery. We split the money evenly the next day. We took a good $160,000 from Westwood Bank. We made $40,000 apiece. That's enough money to stay level for a few months. After things cool down, I could start investigating my father's murder. I might have to break into the building because it's closed down. It shut down a week ago. Money had to be made to keep the place open, and the workers had to get paid. That's my best guess. I would've taken over the business if I had the money. That place was like a second home. I've worked in that building plenty of times with my father. I could run it with my eyes close. Forty thousand dollars is not a lot of money. I could get by for a year if I spent it wisely. I remember my father would blow forty grand in five minutes.

He bought expensive jewelry for my mother or something valuable to sit around the house. That's how fast money could be wasted if not careful. My lifestyle is not the same, and I'm not a kid anymore. I have to care for my mother now. The money is not enough to pay someone full time to take care of her. I'm not about to rob another bank just to bring her home. I have to figure out another way very soon. Maybe I could start a small business? I have to do something. My mother was still in the same mental state. She was staring at the rose bush without any facial expression. No emotions. Why didn't she recognize me? I'm not sure if she realizes I'm her son. I couldn't tell if she was gaining or losing progress. When I looked in her eyes, it was the same vacant stare. I'm not close to my mother the same as I was with my father. The love I feel is absolutely the same. I checked her visitations. There wasn't anyone else on the list besides me. No Abel. I don't understand why he wouldn't visit our mother. He was closer to her than me. I thought he would live at the hospital. He could be embarrassed by her or had to go back to school? His situation doesn't matter. Our mother is more important. He could've visited her at least once. My father told us to take care of her, no matter the case. Abel wasn't holding up his end of the bargain. Driving back to the apartment was hard. My mind kept traveling back and forth between everything that had happened in my life up until now. I thought mostly about the bank robbery. I'm good so far. It's been three days, and nobody had kicked down our door. I won't worry myself to death. If they decide to come, then so be it. At this point in my life, I don't give a damn. I opened the apartment door, and a mouthwatering smell hit my nose. Kim must have hooked up some dinner. I sat the keys on the kitchen counter and looked in the microwave. Chicken, cool. I need something in my stomach. I haven't eaten all day. I pressed the timer on the microwave. The door to the bedroom was slightly open, and I peeped inside. Kim was sound asleep. After I finished tearing down the chicken, I relaxed on the sofa, and my phone began to ring. Unknown? I picked it up anyway. It could be someone calling from the hospital or information regarding my father. "Hello." "Kane," The voice sounded strange. "Who's this and what do you want?" The person on the line sounded like radio. "Just call me, The Planner." He said. "I have a great opportunity for you." "What kind of opportunity are you talking about?" I told him. I wasn't about playing any games with this guy. I just robbed a bank, so I have to keep my head in the game. This could be a setup. "A five-million-dollar opportunity." He responded. Five million dollars, damn. I had no choice but to listen. "You have my attention."

Chapter 40
FEAR OF MAN

I got off the phone with the guy who called himself The Planner. I have some serious thinking to do and only three days to make a decision. He wants me to steal a diamond from the Atlanta Museum. How in the hell am I supposed to pull that off? I mean, I successfully robbed a bank. That's not the same as breaking into a museum. That's a whole new ballgame. I had to consider the offer, a night worth of work for five million dollars. Damn, that's a lot of cash. The first thing that came to mind was everything I could do with the money. I can get my mother out of the mental hospital and have her cared for at home. Kim and I can buy a home far away from here and just live. I can hire a private investigator to find my father's killer. I don't know what I'll do if I caught the person. The way my mind had been acting on its own, it won't be pleasant. I planned to kill whoever is responsible. I used to think my mind had a limit. After everything that had taken place as of late, that's not true. I'm scared of myself. The diamond stayed on my mind the entire night. The Planner said the best time to steal it would be Tuesday night. That's three days from now. The security will be light, and the diamond will be out of its case for cleaning. I'll have a ten-minute window before the rock is back inside the security case. The cleaning process is done at 2 am, so this would definitely be a night job. That works in my favor. The Planner told me everything I needed to know about the museum as if he worked at the place for years. He explained every detail. I had a mental floorplan in my mind. The only thing that worried me was him. There are billions of people in the world. Why did he choose me? Damn, this could be a setup, but somewhere in my mind, I knew that wasn't the circumstance. I'll have a conversation with Kim in the morning. She'll know what to do in this situation. She's the smart one. I won't tell Smoke and the rest of the crew until I literally check out the diamond. I have three days. Tomorrow, Kim and I will go to the museum. Everything, The Planner mentioned, I have to see for myself, then I'll make my final decision. I walked into the dining room and sat at the table. I stared at the plant for a long time. I thought about how Kim rolled some buds in a blunt. She was sleeping, so I had to roll it on my own. I'm not about to wake her up for something stupid. I felt relaxed when I smoked. The weed made my mind clear, and somehow it enhanced my focus ability. I found a blunt. I carefully split it in two on the kitchen counter. I dumped the guts in the trash and made my way back to the table. I picked two good buds from the plant. I broke them down with my fingers just like I saw Kim. Wow, I never thought that I would use drugs. I saw myself playing a professional sport or running my father's business. Basketball, I was good. Football, I was a monster. Track, I was considered a phenom. I actually miss being in high school, playing in big games, and the fans cheering for our team to win. The rival games were the best. We'll be in the second half of a football game and might be down seven points with two minutes to go in the fourth. They would have the ball. No chance to win the game. The defense would make the stop, and the crowd would go wild. We'll score a miracle touchdown, and the crowd would cheer for us to go for a two-point conversion to seal the victory. Game over. Those were the days. I managed to roll up the blunt. It's not the best, but good enough. I got super high. Now, I was playing a new game with the diamond, five million, and... The Planner.

Chapter 41
ABEL'S CREW

bel sat at his computer in the mansion. He thought, there is no way in hell the diamond is worth five million dollars. Why would The Planner pay that amount instead of doing it himself? The Planner was getting something out of the deal, or he could be a private collector. Abel formed new plans. He thought. After I steal this diamond, I have a plan for The Planner. Does he think he can buy me for a cheap five million dollars? Well, surprise, surprise. This diamond will solidify my rank as a dealer in the black market. That's where I'll gain real power by using the diamond to my advantage. I'm sure there will be prominent clientele. Major buyers with power will want the diamond. Network with these buyers and gain their trust. I will be more trustworthy to buy, sell, and trade with them. Then work my way through the government. The diamond means nothing. What matters most is power. If The Planner cannot meet my demands, I'll have to kill him. He smirked at the thought. He typed a very important message to a college roommate that goes by the code name, Snake Eater. Abel knew he would need help with the diamond heist. Snake has the same kind of twisted mind as himself. He is also brilliant, but not as smart as Abel. They both compared their great minds at a science competition, and Abel barely won. Afterward, Abel told Snake every flaw he had with his project. Snake went to his room and stayed up all night, correcting them. Abel was right. He gawked at Abel's intelligence, and the next day they became friends. Later they became roommates and best friends. They planned to gain power together and move up in the world as high-profile criminals. Use their power to take over the government and then the White House. Abel finished the message. This is the opportunity we have been waiting for. Sincerely, Mind Bandit. Abel only dealt with people that have a high IQ. He doesn't surround himself with people he thinks are knuckleheads. The main reason he wasn't close to Kane. Snake was more of a brother. He sent another message to a guy who is the smartest person who ever attended Harvard. A guy he met while traveling to their school for a debate competition. He goes by the code name, BAM. Meaning, Brilliant At Mind. Abel defeated BAM by answering the final question in a debate competition between their schools. They won the state title because of it. Abel answered 41 out of his team's 51 questions. Abel single handedly tore Harvard apart. BAM knew right then Abel was the smartest 16-year-old kid that he has ever met in his life. After they lost, he exchanged numbers with Abel. Later, Abel found out BAM hated the government with a passion. They planned to expose the powers that be by corrupting them using blackmail. Abel needed a guy on the team with his capabilities. He finished the message. The government awaits. Sincerely, Mind Bandit. He sent a message to the only person who is a knucklehead, but not for being unintelligent. The reason was for not having a desire to excel in school, a computer mastermind that goes by the code name, Ali. Meaning, A Living Intelligence. That's what he told Abel his name meant. Ali's hacking ability is beyond anyone Abel has ever met. His mind was sucked inside a computer like the Matrix. That's what Abel loved about him. He can hack into anything and everything involving data. Ali's mind is made of cyber cells. He finished the message. Secret Intel, you'll love it. Sincerely, Mind Bandit. He messaged the only person he thought was smart enough to have his children, Gina. She told Abel her name stood for, Genius In Numerous Accusations. Gina is the smartest girl at Yale, and he loved that she is on the debate team. She wants to be the first woman president and told him she'll kill whoever to achieve her dream. Another girl at the school was ahead of her for the final spot on the team. The girl was found beaten to death. Gina told Abel what happened because she has feelings for him. Abel never revealed her secret to anyone. He finished the message. Here's your chance to be that person. Sincerely, Mind Bandit.

Chapter 42
MUSEUM WORK -KANE-

"Wake up, Kane." I heard a voice calling my name in my sleep. "Get up. You fell asleep on the couch." I slightly opened my eyes and saw Kim standing over me. I didn't have any idea what was going on. "I'm up. I'm up." I said drowsily. "You slept on the couch last night." She said. "You didn't make it to the room. Did something happen? I was beginning to worry when I woke up this morning. Is everything alright?" I looked at Kim. She had a worried look on her face like she had been up all night. I replayed what happened in my mind before I answered. I still felt slightly high. I looked at the living room table and saw somewhat of the blunt I tried to roll. Yesterday was slowly coming back to me. I asked Kim for a glass of water while I gathered my thoughts. I was at the hospital working with my mother before I came home. When I walked through the door, Kim was sound asleep in the bedroom. I wanted to tell her about The Planner. She must have worried herself to sleep, wondering if I was ok. Something told me to call home and let her know everything was fine. After the bank robbery, the police were still looking for the suspects. I don't blame her one bit. She lost me for two years, and I couldn't imagine what that multiplied by ten would do to her. She hurried back with a glass of fresh, ice-cold water. She asked if my mother was fine. I drank half a glass in one gulp and caught a brain freeze. Damn, they break me down every time. After the mini torture was over, I remembered the phone call with The Planner, breaking into the museum, the diamond, and five mill for stealing it. I would've never thought in a million years I come across something this insane. "She's fine, thanks for asking." I looked Kim in the eyes seriously and told her to have a seat. She had a worried look on her face. I needed to ease her anxiety. I could tell she was anxious to hear the news. I reached over to the ashtray and grabbed the blunt. I passed it to her after taking a puff. I asked her to calm down. That reminded me of how she handles my problems when I'm the one in a tough situation. I'm trying to figure out how to explain the phone call and the diamond, how I feel pressured to jump right back out there and commit another crime. The diamond heist is far worse, and I'm considering it. I faced her and couldn't help noticing the innocent look on her face. While smoking last night, I thought about a few things. I felt like I was pulling her along with me, dragging her into a life of crime. Am I ruining her life? We'll be on America's Most Wanted. That's how I'm beginning to feel if this keeps up. What about starting a family? I thought about it, and not even that could change my mind about this one. Only Kim can stop this from happening. I was convinced The Planner was legit and not trying to set me up. "Someone called me last night." She had a concerned look on her face when she asked, "Who? Was it the police? Kane, don't tell me you have to turn yourself in and go back to jail? I don't know what I'll do without you." "No," I assured her. "It's not the police. I'm not going back to jail. I'll die before I leave you and go back to that place. It's something else. A person called about stealing a diamond." "Who?" She asked. "Steal what diamond?" I waved my hand. "Let me finish telling you everything, Ok?" She nodded. "Ok then, there's this guy who changed his voice when he called me out nowhere. He didn't tell me his real name. He goes by a code name, The Planner." A confused look took over her face. "He spoke about a diamond at the Atlanta Museum. He wants me to steal it. He said, I have three days, or he'll cancel the deal. I need to make a move on Tuesday night. If successful, I'll get five million dollars." "Did he sound legit?" "He was convincing enough," I told her. "After seriously thinking about it. I don't think the police would come like that. They would pick me up in a heartbeat if they knew I had something to do with the bank robbery. It would be stupid to send me on another mission that could get me killed. That would be blood on their hands. Why step up a level when they could get me to hit another bank? I'm sure you agree?" Kim stood and stared at me for a moment before speaking. "Let's check out the museum."

Chapter 43
CHECK OUT TIME

Abel put his genius mind to work. He had a few things on his to do list. The first thing he wanted to do was check his emails to see if his college friends responded. He checked the first message. It was from Snake Eater. On the way to you. Good, he thought. That's one member on the team. Snake is the smartest out of the bunch. Abel knew there was no limit with him. His twisted mind is like his own. He checked the second message. It was from BAM. I wouldn't miss it for the world. Another one, he thought. That makes two. BAM will be great for the team. He clicked forward to the next message. He needed this person the most but could manage. He opened the message from Ali. I'm sending my mind your way. A computer hacker was great. Ali is on his way, along with Snake and BAM. He'll make it easier to control the security system by infiltrating the computer's brain. He checked the final message. It was from the person he knew would work the hardest out of the bunch even if she had to kill. He opened the message from Gina. Poison them all. Someone will definitely be murdered. She'll probably leave a trail of bodies, he thought. All four of my team members are in place. They will be arriving tomorrow. In two days, we'll make our move. "Diamond for five million just shot up to thirty-five million. That's my final offer." He muttered to himself. The second thing on his to do list was research. The Planner filled him in on everything about the diamond. Abel never went by what people told him. He found out on his own. Nothing is better than gathering information on your own. That's what he lives by, making his own rules. He's smart, brilliant. The only thing that matters is power. That's what it boils down to, power. The diamond and the money are not a concern. A small sacrifice to control the world. The government, then work his way up to the President's office. Not be him, but control him even though he's smart enough to run for the position. He plans to friend nearby countries and open a worldwide market of blackmail of his own. Gain as many prominent leaders under his control. He'll be the leader of an unwanted war. Eventually, he'll have enough power to shape his new world order. He got up from his computer. He grabbed the keys to his parents, ZO6. Cool way to ride, he thought. He made his way over to the Atlanta Museum. He parked the car and got out. He stood in front of the building. "There better be a diamond in there." He stepped through the front door and paid the toll. Got his ticket from the young lady at the booth, then grabbed a tour guide from the front counter. He opened it and scanned through the mini guide. He didn't want to waste any time looking at nothing else besides what he come for. "Bingo." He said as he found the diamond. "The African Black diamond." The diamond is black? He thought before continuing to read the description. After he finished the section, he turned the page. There was a picture of a huge black diamond. What a prize. I bet there are a lot of buyers who would love to get their filthy hands on this. Especially, enemies who pose a threat. The cost of war is not cheap. The Africans would probably do anything to get this back home. After following the map, he stood in front of some ancient paintings. He looked at the map again, confused. "Oh." He turned around and saw a beautiful black diamond inside a concealed case. He approached the case. The diamond looked amazing. It was the most beautiful piece he had ever seen. Suddenly, his time was cut short. He spotted an unwanted presence through the glass case. What in the hell is he doing here, he thought. He ducked back over by the paintings just to be safe. "Kane?" He muttered to himself before disappearing into a herd of tourists.

Chapter 44
DOUBLE CHECKOUT -KANE-

Kim and I pulled up to the museum. She is braver than I initially thought. Inside, this woman is a little criminal. Her whole mentality changed when I told her about the diamond and the five million. She said to me if we're crazy enough to rob a bank for $160,000 and risk it all. She didn't see why not consider checking out the museum. On the way, we talked about different ways to enter the building. We didn't have a clue how to pull off the heist. It was a good thing we came to check out the scenery just in case we took the job. Being inside the museum might give me a second opinion about accepting The Planner's deal. Right now, I'm at the point where this entire situation is too good to be true. We're talking five million dollars. He could've hired a professional with that kind of dough. We got out of the vehicle, and I blocked the money out of my mind. I have to focus and find out everything I could about this place while I'm here. I walked to the front of the car, where I met Kim. She grabbed my hand, and we walked together while holding hands. We reached the front of the museum. "Atlanta Museum," I muttered to myself while looking at the sign in front. The building was massive and people were everywhere. Children were leading their parents inside with excited looks on their faces. I always wanted to come here as a child. I never would've guessed it would be to rob the place. We entered through the front, and my mind was already beginning to work. I took mental snapshots of everything from the parking lot to the front door. I stored every detail in my mind. My father used to say I have a good memory. Use it well because if you don't, it won't work hard enough to remember anything. It'll slowly become a fruit, and recalling yesterday would be a task. Ok, that was some good inspiration to get my mind working. Who wants a big giant fruit sitting up there for a brain? Kim paid the nice lady at the toll booth. She gawked at me like I was a famous person and began to blush. I thought, oh damn. Kim caught her staring, and I turned away, trying not to cause trouble. Too late. Kim looked at the lady with a scary expression on her face. I think she just woke the devil. "Excuse you," Kim said with an attitude. "I don't appreciate you staring at my man like you can't wait to suck his dick." "I'm sorry." The lady at the ticket booth replied. "He looks like someone I saw a minute ago." I was stuck in the middle of a catfight and was lost for words. I didn't know how to respond. This is the first time two women fought over me. It's kind of exciting. I thought about what we were here for. I grabbed Kim by the arm and pulled her away from what could have turned into a big problem. Kim continued threatening the lady as I pulled her away. "You know what I'm talking about, bitch!" She yelled back at the woman. "You better not be here when I get back. You hear me, or that's an ass kicking you can count on." "Kim, come on. Baby." I pleaded with her. "Just forget about it. I don't want you to go to jail. Come on, look at all these people watching us. Think about these kids." I heard the lady at the toll booth say, "Oh my God, she's crazy." When I got this unfamiliar person a safe distance, I released my grip on her arm. She looked at me hard, staring into my eyes as if she fell in love all over again. Then her demeanor changed. Who is this new person I'm with? "Kim-" I started, but didn't get a chance to finish my sentence. She slapped me upside the head, and as she walked away, I heard her say. "I saw you looking at her. You're not getting any tonight." I stood there dumbfounded and couldn't help but smile. Our love had grown since the first day I met her on the track field. Kim was willing to fight and go to jail for someone looking at me wrong. I'm her man and she's my woman. I would've done the same over her without thinking about it. I caught up and hugged her from behind. I kissed her and said, I'm sorry. She smiled and we continued walking while holding hands. We turned a corner and the diamond popped out in our faces. Damn. It's astonishing. I real masterpiece. I noticed a man gawking at it through its glass case. He suddenly reacted to me. Man, he looked just like... Abel. I pulled Kim by the hand and hurried over. The guy had vanished. I thought I was losing my mind. Who knows, maybe I'm becoming someone else? A person who's not like my father.

Chapter 45

SMOKE, MY DREAD
HEAD FRIEND

We were back at the apartment after leaving the museum. The diamond is no doubt a beautiful piece of work, and the damn thing looks more like a thirty-million-dollar grab. I'm not picky, and I don't have anybody who wants to buy it. I considered the five million as a very good settlement. I mean, who wouldn't love five million dollars for working one night? That's like hitting the lottery. Not to mention, tax free. Kim went into the bedroom. My eyes walked with her into the room. I got up when I heard her turn on the shower. Sex was on my mind, and I crept into the room. The bathroom door was wide open and saw her perfect body through the steam. I slipped out of my clothes and eased into the bathroom. She was singing and never saw me sneak inside. Kim has a super sexy body. If she were a model, she would be rich. Just looking at her made me hard. She got surprised when I grabbed her by the waist from behind. "Oh my-" She yelped. I shushed her. She tried to turn around and I didn't let her. I pinned her against the shower wall and began playing with her area. She got wet and it wasn't from the water. I inserted my manhood inside her and she instantly began to moan. It felt so good inside Kim. Actually, unbelievable. I don't care to be with another woman. I only need her. I got aggressive and pounded her hard from the back while holding her by the hips. Her ass is a perfect round apple shape. My pelvis slapped against her ass with every pump. Water splashed in between making a sound of its own. "Oh, Kane." She moaned with pleasure. "I'm coming, baby." Kim moans turned me on. She sounded seductive, and it made me want to go harder. After ten more minutes of absolute pleasure. She came three more times. I began to feel a sensation crawl up my legs, and the rush made me weak in the knees. I was deep inside. "Oh, shit." I groaned. The feeling was extraordinary. Finally, I released inside of her. She's mine. We belong together, and one day I will marry her. I pulled out and exhaled. She turned around and gave me a passionate kiss. Her eyes said she loved me to death. Especially, having unprotected sex and releasing in her without questioning me. "Who's not getting none tonight?" "You talking shit?" She smiled. "The next time it'll be a week. Now get out so I can clean myself up." She pushed me out of the shower. "Yeah, a'ight. We'll see." I said coolly before getting shoved out. She went back to singing, and I grabbed a towel and dried myself off. Usually, that'll put me to sleep, but I still have some things to take care of and don't have much time. I need to start making moves right now. I had a plan for the diamond heist. We had to give the weapons back to Redd, unfortunately. He had to place them back in his father's gun case before he realized they were gone. That's one thing I need to do, get a few weapons and some C4. I didn't have any idea where to find explosives. This is Atlanta and somebody will have it or could direct me to the right person. I plan to get into the museum from the sewer. The Planner didn't think of that route when we spoke. I rather take a path no one else knew about in case something popped off. There was a manhole outside of the museum. I noticed it on the way in when Kim and I scoped out the place. I plan to use the C4 to blow the floor out from underneath the restroom at precisely 2 am. That's when The Planner said the security system would be down for ten minutes to clean the diamond. We'll make our way through the museum, and hopefully, the explosion won't be loud enough to alarm them. I had some kind of a decoy for the upfront security guards. The Planner said there would be two working at the front desk. The best idea I could think of was having Smoke play drunk and fall against the front glass to gain their attention. He's good at acting. Smoke was incredible when he acted in our school plays, and I'm sure he can mimic the same performance. I'll be working underground in the sewer with Redd and Bear, Kim will be the driver this time. I need Bear to be a bear. If something goes down, we will need the extra muscle. Redd will guard the passageway. I can count on him after how well he handled the bank job. One thing I have to get for this job is some kind of transmitter. We need to communicate with each other by any means necessary. Communication is key. Day one, I'll get the equipment. Day two, I'll go over the plan with them. That's if they decided to roll with me on this one. Day three, we'll hit the museum. That's the only way I see it. Luckily, The Planner had everything in order for us, or this job wouldn't be possible. That $40,000 would be long gone in a year, and we need a long-term plan. This was it. I will offer them $500,000 apiece, and that'll leave Kim and I with 3.5 million dollars. That's absolutely enough money for us to live peacefully. I called my best friend, Smoke. He agreed to meet at the apartment and made it in thirty minutes. I told him about everything that went down. I never told him about the five million, just the five hundred thousand he'll make for the job. He agreed and never asked about my pay. He's the kind of friend who was down to ride no matter what, as I would for him. He's still grieving over his grandmother. I saw it all over his face, and I wanted to speak on it but chose to leave it alone. I knew he already paid for his grandmother's surgery. In due time, she'll be fine, and I'll get the old Smoke back. I told him we need guns for this job. He knew a kid who hit a gun store in Atlanta and was selling them for a low price out of his trunk. I didn't ask how he knew the kid and he told me anyway. He was downtown shopping for his uncle's birthday when the kid approached him. He finished the story, and the kid gave him the impression that he was legit. We got to Atlanta in an hour and met with the kid. We followed him to a spot in a nearby neighborhood. He popped the trunk of an old Buick. "Damn," I muttered. This kid has a military of his own. Everything I could think of was in the trunk. I asked how much for the weapons I wanted to purchase and about the C4, welcome to ATL baby. He said. "I got the quiet kind, bro." Great, I was reaching for the money when my heart stopped from the sound of gunfire. I thought we were getting jacked. I ducked in reaction to the fire. I was still alive. I notice Smoke standing with the 9mm Redd had let us use for the bank heist. I shot my vision to the kid selling the weapons. Dead. Smoke killed him. Smoke began to cry while speaking to me. "My grandmother didn't make it, Kane. She's dead man, dead." I couldn't comprehend how Smoke felt. All I know is we have to get the hell out of here. I almost went down for murder once, and I'm not about to go through that again. I got down on the kid. I saw him put the keys in his left pocket after popping the trunk. I made sure not to touch the body more than I had to. I found the keys without any problem. "Smoke, lets bounce." He just stood there watching the kid lost in thought. Fuck. "Smoke, snap out of it. We have to get to fuck out of here." I grabbed him by the arm and jerked the shit out of him, and he came back to life. "Kane I... I killed him." He stammered. "Fuck that, let's ride." I pushed him into the old Buick. Hopefully, this piece of shit still runs. I jumped into the driver seat and tried to start the car. Nothing. Fuck, fuck, fuck. I tried it again. Nothing. How in the hell did he rob a gun store in this piece of shit? I banged on the steering wheel out of frustration. I tried again, and this time it started. "Hell yeah." I put the car in reverse and ran over the guy. Fuck it, he's dead, and it was the only way out of the parking space. I heard Smoke mumbling about jail. I drove the vehicle a mile down the road and parked around the back of a vacant building. "Smoke, come on." We left everything and walked back to his car. We didn't park in the neighborhood, so we were straight. I got the keys from him and drove back to the Buick after checking out the scene. Clear. I parked next to the car and popped both trunks. I loaded the bags of weapons in our trunk. I ripped a piece of cloth I found in Smoke's trunk and placed it in the gas tank of the Buick. I made sure it was long enough so I could drive away in time. I got back in the car. Smoke's mind had drifted to another place. At least that's how he appeared to me. I cranked the car without saying a word. "I don't wanna go to jail, man." He finally spoke. I looked at him seriously. "That's not the plan." I put the car in gear, burning out the tires while speeding off just before the old Buick exploded.

Chapter 46
THE KID -JORDAN-

Wow, these guys look like a bunch of savage predators. I was sitting in the back office of the department. It's more like the video room. Agents came back here to view footage of suspects. It's been several days, and I'm just getting around to viewing the bank heist. I have been in the video room for three hours studying footage caught on the bank's security cameras. I noticed one thing in particular about these guys. They all wore their hair in dreads, just like the Atlanta policewoman mentioned to the reporter. These guys are sonic fast. After watching the film, I noticed the shortest member of the robbers never left the bank's door. He stayed in position surveying the scene like some kind of guard dog. I figured that was his part in the robbery since he never attempted to move. From another angle, I noticed two more men with the same hairstyle. They moved swiftly through the bank. They came into view where a security guard positioned by the vault. The guard attempted to close it but was unsuccessful. One of the masked men made it to the older man in the nick of time and stopped him right before the vault door shut. The largest of the three men team gun butt the guard with a pistol from behind. Cheap fucking shot. He propped the security officer in front of the vault. It was hard to get a view of the suspect because of the camera. Although, I could make out his body. He hopped onto the counter and walked down the tellers. I paused the footage right on the guy. I wanted to meet this guy and see what the hell he was thinking. He moved like a badass from a movie. This guy was like an action hero, bad guy, in a bank heist film. You knew he was on the wrong side but wanted to root for him anyway. He had the leadership role down pat. The way he moved his weapon by cautiously waving everyone down. I presume he was the leader of this pack of wild animals. He appeared to be over six feet tall. His dreads draped down to his chest, and he was well built. I wouldn't want to get into a one on one with this guy on my best day. The black mask covering his face made him look even more ferocious. I sat there staring at the suspect, and he began to look somewhat familiar. I needed a moment to think. I got up and walked over to the drink machine right outside the door. I put the little change I had left in the machine. Suddenly, I heard all kinds of commotion coming from behind me. "What the hell is going on?" I muttered to myself before turning around. I heard the machine drop my drink. My body wouldn't turn around to grab it. I was trying to comprehend what was taking place. I saw Rick through the ruckus. I hurried over and grabbed him by the arm. "Rick, what's going on?" I asked. "It's been a murder in Montage Embry Hills." He looked at me like there was something else to say. I let go of his arm. "Murder?" I asked. "Yeah and get this?" He said with excitement. "A person called in ten minutes ago and said that the suspects wore dreads." An adrenaline rush shot through my body. "They possibly could be our bank robbers." I told him. "Exactly, that's what I'm thinking. They could still be somewhere in the area." He suggested. I looked at the clock. The crime happened thirteen minutes ago, ten more to get to the location. That's more than enough time to flee the scene. "Perhaps, let's get a move on." We made it in the time I expected, ten minutes. The EMT's were already on the scene, and there were bystanders outside their apartments. I overheard a few complaints from the residents. Rick and I walked over for a closer view of the victim. I heard one cry out. "He was a good kid." Another said. "That kid wouldn't harm anybody." They kept going on and on. Finally, the worst of the complaints. "Fuck'em. I'm glad he's dead. He used to beat on my sister, the piece of shit!" I finally made it to the victim. I crouched down next to the body and put on a pair of latex gloves. I pulled back the sheet. Damn, the kid looked at least nineteen years old. He had a babyface. Dead, three to the chest. I covered the body and removed my gloves. I thought to myself for a short moment. These dread headed Indians are making things interesting, and I love it.

Chapter 47
ONE DAY LEFT -KANE-

I woke up the next morning with a little headache. I went to the bathroom and found some Advil. I popped three of them. I was up all night with Smoke trying to get him to stop panicking over the murder. What's done is done. It is what it is. There's no bringing the kid back. Finally, I got through to him. We talked a little about his grandmother's death and how he felt about going through with the diamond heist. He told me his grandmother died an hour before he got to the hospital. Her heart failed on her. He didn't get the chance to speak to her before she left this world. That hurt him the most. She raised him, and death took her before he told her goodbye. I felt where he was coming from. I reminded him of my father's death and how I wasn't able to say goodbye. Just thinking about it made me emotional. Tears spilled from Smoke's eyes for his grandma. I had to be strong for both of us. We have to get through this situation. He said he has to be involved with the heist. He needs the $500,000. He planned to take a trip away from the drama. I told him that was a good idea, and maybe Kim and I would tag along. Honestly, I wanted to watch him and make sure he wasn't suicidal. He welcomed us to join him on vacation. I could only imagine why he killed that kid. It's hard losing someone you love. He probably snapped, and paying the kid was not an option. We left the kid there to die. That's not the Smoke I know, but I would still do anything for him. We had to flee the scene when I realized what had happened. We needed the guns and the C4. I'm trying to figure out what to do with the rest of the weapons. I'll probably sell them for a low price. I need to avoid adding a gun store robbery and a murder to my list of recent criminal activity. Damn, every single day, I'm becoming more of a bad person. When we got back to the apartment, I stayed up all night talking to Smoke. That's what real friends do for one another in times of need. I left the bathroom and went to the living room. Smoke was asleep on the couch. He had to be terrified of the cops coming for him. It's easy to be paranoid after all the shit he went through with his grandma, the bank robbery, and murdering a kid in cold blood. I thought my problems were piling up. Smoke is doing a hell of a job. His mind had to be exhausted. He was in a deep sleep. I had no choice but to wake him. We had to get everything I had planned done today. First, we'll unload the gun and move them inside the apartment. It's not a good idea to ride around with a trunk full of felonies. Second, I'll go over my plan with Redd and Bear. They were unaware of the diamond, and I decided not to tell them about the murder. I rather keep that business to myself. Especially since I'm involved, they'll be safe from the law if they knew nothing. I'm leaning towards not telling Kim. Even though Kim and Smoke have known each other since middle school, they're like family. That'll be on him if he wants to let her know. The only reason I would say anything is because we don't keep secrets. They will ruin your relationship. She'll wonder why I didn't mention it if Smoke told her before we had that conversation. That's my only dilemma. I woke Smoke so we could get the day started. I gave him a change of clothes, a rag, and a towel to wash. After he finished, we unloaded the trunk. His mind was more clear than it was yesterday, good. Afterward, I placed a call to Redd and Bear. It's time to put them on game. I need to know if they're down. I only have one day left. No more shitting around. Five mill on the line. Time to work.

Chapter 48
THE INTELLIGENCE CLUB

Abel waited in his parent's Z06 at the Hartsfield Jackson Atlanta International Airport. He rolled down the window halfway, tossed out a cigarette butt, and checked his watch. His college friend will be arriving at any minute. The rest of his counterparts will arrive later in the afternoon. He felt great considering his current situation. He has the mansion all to himself. His brother is out of his hair, along with his mother weeping every ten minutes. He felt relieved after putting her in a mental hospital. The old hag was beginning to work his nerves. Anymore crying out of her would've sealed her fate, just like her husband. He chose not to end her worthless life, and surprisingly, the next day, she had a mental breakdown. He thanked God for answering his prayers. Killing his mother wasn't on his to do list, but she was leaving him no other options. The diamond, he thought. The power he would gain after possessing the African Black Diamond. That piece will place him where he needs to be, along with his father's notebook. The notebook is the key to his immaculate plan. The diamond will act as a pawn. He'll get the best offer, if not what he desires from The Planner. He drove the sports car a little farther up the road. He watched traffic move in and out of the airport's pickup area and noticed a guy with a baldhead, hauling his luggage. He smirked at his college buddy, Snake. He drove the vehicle closer to the curve. Snake continued through the crowd and approached the sidewalk. The man even looked like a genius. Abel rolled down the passenger side window after pulling up the car. "Excuse me, sir," He joked. "I'm looking for a reptile that likes to eat mice?" Snake smiled. "It's been a long time, my friend. I see you still have the same corny jokes." "Hey, only a knucklehead got time to come up with funnier jokes." Abel popped the trunk. "Back," Signaling for Snake to put his suitcase in the trunk. Snake shut the trunk after he finished and got in the passenger seat. "You bought yourself a very nice sports car, my friend." "Oh, this is nothing. I stole it from a mentally ill woman." Abel smirked after witnessing a confused facial expression from his friend. "That's not a joke." He revved the ZO6 and burnt out from the pickup lane. They talked about old times at the college and how much they wanted to take over the government and the White House. They stopped to grab a bit to eat, where they talked a little about chess. They love challenging each other at the sport. They would have long, intense battles. Whenever one would lose is how they solidified who was more intelligent. Out of the 125 games played. Snake beat Abel the first ten games, but Abel had a higher win total. After they finished eating and chatting about who was better, they made their way to what Abel called his mansion. Abel parked in front of his enormous home. "Wow, I was unaware you were a millionaire." Snake said. "I see why you never made it back to school. Who needs school when you have your own?" He referred to the mansion as being big enough to be a school. "True," Abel said. "And I don't have to tell you who I had to kill to get it." "You did the right thing." Snake assured. "Kill for self interest. That's my model." Abel popped the trunk and Snake grabbed his suitcase. They entered the home. Abel assumed Snake had never been in a house this big. He gawked at everything his eyes captured. Finally, after getting his guest settled. Abel wanted to go over every single detail involving the heist. Snake was aware he came for a secret mission. Abel told him everything about the diamond and the guy who offered the job. "The Planner." "The Planner?" Snake thought, what a crazy name. "Is that what this guy is calling himself?" "That's correct, my friend." "That's stupid." Snake said. "He has to be aware we know the diamond is worth more than a cheap five million."

"Of course, the diamond is worth more than what he offered. I visited the museum myself to check out the rock. It's a beautiful piece of work. I did some research on the piece, and it has an estimated value of one hundred million. We'll settle for 35 million from The Planner and if he chooses not to accept my new offer. We'll travel to Africa." Abel heard his phone ringing after two hours of chatting with Snake about a plan. He picked up the line. It was BAM. "I'm at the airport along with Ali and Gina." "I'll send my limo." Actually, my dead father's limo. He began to laugh on the inside.

Chapter 49
SEWER WORK -KANE-

"Ok, everyone clear on what they need to do?" I asked my team. We were moments away from pulling off the biggest heist in history. This job will make me a rich man beyond my wildest dreams. That's what I'm praying for. I'll put the five million dollars in an offshore bank account somewhere in Jamaica. Kim and I will take a nice vacation. The feds would be all over my case if the money were deposited in my American account. That will definitely raise a red flag. I want to avoid federal time by any means necessary. "I'm ready to get the show on the road when you are." Smoke said. He sipped on a beer to get his breath smelling right for the job. "Let's do it," Bear said. "No time to sleep." "This can go two ways," Redd spoke up. "And I'm ready for both." "I'm ready, my love." Kim said with her eyes pent on me. "Jamaica, here we come." "Good, everyone's ready." I said to all of them. "Now, once we are in the field. There's no turning back. Whatever you have on your mind, get it off. Your leg, grandma, sleeping disorder, your criminal boyfriend, or dead father. All of that shit needs to be turned off. Our minds need absolute focus. No mistakes. Bear, be a bear. Smoke, be on your best act. Redd, be on guard, and very alert. Kim, drive the hell out of the car when we get back. Ok, it's 1:15 am. We need to be on the move." We broke from the apartment. Kim will drive Smoke's Audi because we need a fast vehicle. We have a change of clothes for partying in the trunk. If we happen to get stopped on the way from the museum, we were coming from the club, just having a good time together out on the town. We're all old high school friends. Kim doesn't drink, and she offered to give everyone a ride home. That's the story we all had in our minds as we drove to the museum. We took the back roads. There were no cops out. That's good for what we're trying to accomplish. We arrived at the museum at approximately 1:45 am. That's fifteen minutes before they remove the diamond from the case. We're on point as of right now. Something I never thought I would have to use again, the black hockey mask slid over my face. The predators want to play. Members of a criminal group dubbed as The Dreads. What I hated and loved was that I'm the leader of this group of devoted friends. We own the night. That's how I felt as we exited the vehicle. "Bear, you have the pry bar?" I asked him.

Bear is the biggest and toughest out of the bunch, and he's the only one with sewer knowledge. His father used to work the sewers for the city before he was promoted. Bear knew how to get around underground better than anyone. His father brought him on a couple of jobs when Bear was kicked off the football team. He needed extra manpower, so he brought his son. I remember Bear mentioning the only thing he hated about the sewers was the smell. "Got it." He said, showing me the tool. "Alright, ready when you are, big man." I replied. Bear went to work on the manhole. He placed the bar in one of the holes and lifted. Nothing. The next, nothing. I was beginning to think there won't be any diamond heist. Bear doesn't know what the hell he's doing. Finally, on the last hole, it popped. Damn, I guess I was wrong. I turned on my flashlight and aimed the light through the hole. I couldn't see anything at the bottom of the sewer. It was completely dark. We could only see what was in line with the light. "Shit water," I muttered to myself. "Any rats down there?" Redd asked. "Man, I don't fuck with rats." "No rats, Redd." I lied to stop him from being paranoid. "Do you think they'll live down there without fresh cheese?" Now stop being a bitch. "Oh, ok." He said. "But if I see one." "Just come on. You won't see anything, I promise." I told him another lie. Redd stayed close to Bear, and we proceeded down the manhole. Bear was our guide, and we followed the pipes to the museum's restrooms. The diamond will be clean on the other side of the building. The goal is not to alarm the workers when we reached our location. I placed a block of C4 on a good spot and radioed Smoke.

Chapter 50
ROOF WORK

Abel looked at his watch. "1:35 am." He muttered. "Ladies and gentlemen, listen up. It's time to take our positions. Do we have everything in order for us to succeed?" "I'm uploading the software to hack into the museum's computer database." Ali continued typing on his laptop. "Yes, I have pistols with silencers attached." Snake placed the weapons in a bag. He was excited to be part of something this big. He kept thinking about how famous they would be if the heist were a success. Tomorrow we will be famous. This will make me a millionaire. I'll have to kill someone to celebrate our victory. Maybe, it'll be someone in the government? He visualized the events taking place in his wicked mind. That'll be nice. "Yes, I have every tool we'll need to enter the museum from above as you ask." BAM opened a bag of equipment for Abel. "Here, everyone gets a watch and a transmitter. We'll need to keep track of time and, of course, communicate. Ali will allow us to have a great signal from the van." He gave out supplies. This is great. Finally, there's something to live for. "I have everything I need." Gina rubbed her hands down her long overcoat, starting from her breasts. Her job is to distract the front desk security guards. She wondered what the police would say after finding their bodies. The cause of death will be unknown until the coroner's report. "Let's get a move on," Abel signaled for everyone to load up inside the van. "We have a diamond to steal." It took them ten minutes to reach the museum. Abel, Snake, and BAM all crept over to the side of the massive building. Gina got to her position. She'll transmit to Ali to move forward, entering phase three. The security cameras will be easier to secure with the guards out of the picture. She's the second part of the masterplan. Ali stayed positioned inside the van. His only job is to hack into the museum's security system through satellite. It will allow him to take control of the cameras to monitor their activity. Eagle eyes for Abel and Snake while they were working through the building. The transmitters will allow communication through each checkpoint. The plan was perfect and Ali enjoyed the challenge. He'll activate part three of the masterplan. Abel grabbed an anchor with a long rope attached to the end. He tossed it to the top of the roof. The anchor locked in a secured position. The rope was safe for them to climb up the side of the building. They wore black clothing to blend in with the night. Abel found the vent The Planner mentioned. BAM handed him a screwdriver. He removed the screws from each corner of the vent's opening and carefully set it to the side. Afterward, he radioed Gina. "Ok, I'm moving into position." Gina said while walking up the street to the museum. She noticed a homeless man in the alley as she passed. He was very drunk and holding a walkie talkie in his hand. A drunk talking into a device like someone will respond. He probably stole it off a kid, she thought. There's a high rate of homeless people in Atlanta, so she paid it no mind and continued to the front entrance of the museum. She put her face to the door and looked through the window. She spotted the guards at the front desk. They appeared to be joking around with each other. She tapped on the glass to get their attention. One of the guards noticed her and walked over. Gina unstrapped her overcoat as he approached the door, revealing her amazing body. The guard was taken by surprise at the sight of an exotic naked woman. He was excited to let her inside. She told him somebody hired a stripper. He lied and said, yes. She held him by the face, and gracefully kissed his lips. She let her coat drop to the floor as he stood there, choking on his own blood. He fell to the floor after a short moment, dead. She approached the other guard before he noticed. He was the second to die after accepting her kiss of death. Both guards were sprawled out on the museum's marble floor lifeless. Her job was done and she radioed Abel and then Ali.

Chapter 51
OTHER MOTIVES -KANE-

"What is your location?" I asked Smoke. I was ready to blow a hole in the floor. This is my first-time using dynamite. The most important thing to remember is clearing out after pressing the red button. I do want to keep my head attached to my shoulders. "I'm in the alley." He confirmed his position. "Continue with phase two of the plan. Make sure to inform me when you're done, cool?" "No problem. I'm on the move." I heard him whisper through the transmitter. We moved to a safe distance. Redd kept crying about rats. I have to stay mentally focused, so I ignored him. My mind was busy at the moment. Under the circumstances, rats are at the bottom of my list. For the next hour, I have to move with a clear head. I had a feeling that things were about to get hectic. I'm beginning to learn to go with my first instinct. "Shit." Smoke spoke into the transmitter. "We have a major problem." Smoke sounded petrified. "Shit, what?" I responded. "What's the problem? You good?" "The guards, man." I heard Smoke sigh through the radio. "They're dead." I instantly switched from calm to paranoid. What the hell is going on? The guards are dead? I need answers. I didn't expect anything like this to happen. "Did you kill them?" I asked seriously. "No, man." He assured me. "They were already dead. It's unbelievable." "Already dead?" I muttered. "Did you see anything?" Redd and Bear locked in on the conversation. Their facial expressions were serious. No one was thinking about rats or being asleep. "No, nothing." He answered. "I was following through with the plan, and when I approached the door to stumble into it, I fell through. It was open. I saw the first guard sprawled out on the ground. I checked his pulse, dead. I crept to the front desk. I walked around, and I tripped over another body. It was the second guard. Man, I'm telling you. Either God's trying to set us up, or someone else is in the building. This is some bullshit." I went through everything in my mind that Smoke mentioned. It's not hard to consider. The Planner had other motives. Two dead guards and the front door open. C'mon, I'm not that crazy. I had to act quickly. "What's your position?" "I'm still at the front desk." He said. "I'm looking at the entire museum through the security cameras." "Ok, don't move." I ordered. "We're coming up." "What's going on?" Redd asked with a concerned look on his face. "Yeah, wassup?" Bear added. "What he say?" I blew by both of them, heading back out the manhole. I can't miss this opportunity. We don't have to blow a hole under the museum. The bad thing is The Planner possibly sent another team. Maybe he thought I wouldn't get the job done. Someone is trying to get their hands on the diamond. I came too far for that to happen. I'm not about to leave without the diamond. I need that money. I had my assumptions, but when it's all said and done. The stone is mine. "C'mon, I'll explain on the way." Time is of the essence. We have to meet Smoke at the front desk. We hurried through the sewer. The sound of water splashed under our boots. It was the same sound soldiers made while running in the rain. I popped the manhole and ran to the entrance. I looked through the glass and saw Smoke at the security desk. I walked through and my feet froze unexpectedly. My mind told them not to take another step. The first guard was in front of me. His body was lifeless. That's strange. I spotted a long overcoat on the floor. Red and Bear finally caught up to me. They were also shocked by the dead guard. We hurried to Smoke. The second guard was behind the desk. Fuck, dead. This was serious and I felt a bit frustrated. I checked the cameras and saw one man prepping the diamond. There was also another person in the building. I saw the killer on camera. Ironically... it was a naked woman.

Chapter 52

THE AFRICAN BLACK DIAMOND

I was on the prowl after viewing the woman on camera. I told Redd to stand guard by the security desk. Someone needed to watch the cameras and the door. If something came up, we would be notified before the situation got hot. I went after the diamond. I doubled checked my Beretta to make sure it was loaded. If this woman was the killer, better safe than sorry, it's not a coincidence that two guards are dead and she's in the building. How? I don't have the slightest clue. I rather not think about what happened. When it comes down to it, she's dangerous. The guards underestimated her, end of story. I revised my plan. Now I have to account for the woman. There's a high chance she's not alone. She possibly could be The Planner's secret weapon. I crept down the hall towards the diamond room with Smoke and Bear close behind. Our weapons were scanning the area. We were ready to get this fucking diamond and get the hell out of the building safely. The mask covering their faces made them appear without emotion. What if one of us had to catch a body? Were they ready for that? Were they my friends or the predators who helped me rob a bank? Hopefully, they'll stay loyal even if that meant murder. I stopped at the end of the hall. I was in proximity to the diamond. The exact spot where I caught up with Kim and hugged her. We have an advantage with Redd monitoring us from the security cameras. I unstrapped my transmitter from my leg. "Redd, what's going on in the diamond room?" I asked. "We're in position to move on the diamond. I don't see the woman. She could be close by." "I don't know what's going on with the security system." Redd said, concerned. "Every time I try to switch the view, the damn thing switches back on the naked woman. She's around the corner from your position, in the same hallway as the diamond. There could be someone monitoring her because it's like the cameras have a mind of their own. I did figure out they switched back after two seconds." I can believe the woman is working with someone. That means somebody is controlling the cameras or the damn things are malfunctioning. We have to be on high alert. If The Planner sent her, she could be even more dangerous than I had initially thought. "Ok, let me know?" "Done," Redd got back to me in ten seconds. "The diamond is being cleaned by one person. It appears to be another man observing him." Good, that's exactly what I need to know. We had to be mistake free from this point on. The game is officially on. I peeped around the corner. I caught a glimpse of the woman's backend before she disappeared into the diamond room. Damn, I had to refocus. She was bad, at least from the back. C'mon, Kane. Stop thinking with your dick. There's a strong possibility this woman is a maniac. Remember the guards? I had to tell myself some words of encouragement. I looked swiftly around the corner a second time, clear. Something told me this situation is not about to be good. I signaled for Smoke and Bear to move cautiously. We began moving closer towards the room, and I peeped inside the door. I saw the woman holding her hands up in a defensive position. The cleaner quickly tried to place the diamond in the case. I wonder how many times they trained for a robbery? The woman hurried toward the case and blocked his attempt to secure the stone. I ducked back into cover and waited. I heard her yell, hand over the diamond. Then one of the men responded, the police are on the way. Fuck, we have to move fast. This is not supposed to be this simple. Neither of the men had a gun. I didn't see any signs of protection. The woman didn't have a pistol unless it's hidden somewhere that I rather not say. But if she did, that will be a hell of a trick. We have the advantage. Three masked men with guns compared to two cleaners and a naked lady. Those odds were great and I'm trying to win. I signaled for Smoke to grab the cleaner by the diamond and Bear the woman. I'll take care of the other worker. I took off. "Don't fucking move." I grabbed the guy and knocked him out. Bear held the smaller woman in arms, she struggled, but couldn't match his amazing strength. Smoke hit the cleaner over the head, and he collapsed to the floor like a weakling, then took the diamond and tossed it to me. I held it up to the light, staring at the fascinating piece. Five mill, baby.

Chapter 53

DIAMOND SHOWDOWN

The diamond is even more alluring out of its holding case. My eyes were captivated by its beauty, and it was hard for me to look away. My future rested in my hands, literally. How many people in the world can actually say that? At the moment, I was one of them. I placed the diamond in my pouch and zipped it shut. Securing the diamond takes priority over any other matter. The man who was cleaning the stone couldn't stop shaking, and I made him lay facedown on the floor. I looked at Bear, holding the naked woman. Her body was enchanting. She could not be underestimated after making it this far. The look on her face told me she wasn't scared. She had shown no signs of being frightened of three masked men with guns. I studied her face while trying to keep my manhood from bulging out of my pants. Kim would kill me right now. I swear, she smirked at me as if I was the one in danger. I told Smoke to keep his gun aimed at her. It's time to find out if she was hired by The Planner. I approached her after slowly lowering my gun. "Who sent you?" If it were The Planner who sent her, then that would mean he didn't trust me to be successful. I wouldn't believe her if she said she acted alone. How ironic, a professional thief robbing the museum on the same day. What are the odds? She could play me or speak the truth. Either way, the diamond belongs to me. "Just give me a kiss and I'll tell you who sent me." She looked serious. A kiss at a time like this? Note to self. She's a psycho. Why in the hell does she want to kiss me? She's trying to trick me into revealing my face, making it easier for her to come after me later. Suddenly, Smoke walked over and lifted his mask. "I'll do it." I blocked his path. "What the fuck are you doing? Put your mask down. There're cameras in the room. This psycho just wants to see your face." He pulled down his mask in a hurry. "My bad," He spoke softly. "Don't worry. My friend is taking care of the cameras. Now come over here and give momma a kiss." She said seductively. "Friend?" I asked. She didn't answer, smiled, and blew a kiss in my direction. I wondered what the hell was her problem? Suddenly, I heard something above our heads, I'm sure of it. "What the fuck now?" I muttered under my breath. I looked upward at the ceiling and I noticed a vent. Everyone in the room froze. We all were locked in on the noise. Nothing, no sound. I must be paranoid. I have what I came for, time to go. I focused on the woman. I contemplated what to do with her. Taking a hostage wasn't a part of the plan, that's kidnapping. Not to mention, Kim wouldn't like the idea of a naked hostage. Fuck, think. My thoughts were interrupted when I suddenly heard muffled gunfire. I swiftly got into cover. I heard Bear yelling out in pain. Smoke started firing at the vent. What the fuck just happened? Somebody was in the ventilation system. A second spray of fire erupted. I saw Bear lying on the floor, holding his massive shoulder. The woman had escaped. I didn't see her anywhere in the room. I crawled over to Bear while covering myself. Smoke yelled. "They're in the vent!" I safely made it to Bear. Damn, he got hit in the shoulder. Blood soaked through his shirt and spilled through the cracks in his fingers. It angered me to see my friend hurt. I reacted and unloaded a couple of rounds towards the vent, hoping to hit whoever shot my buddy. My heart began racing faster than ever. I told Smoke to provide cover fire while I helped Bear. Smoke shot at the vent multiple times. There was no chance for the gunman to return fire. I got Bear on his feet. "Let's get the hell out of here." We raced from the room. Smoke followed behind. I radioed Kim when we were safely in the hall. "Pull around." Redd had his gun aimed down the hall and lowered it when he saw us. "He straight? I saw what happened." He hurried over to help. "He's been shot," I told him. "Get the door." My mind focused on getting out of the museum alive. I don't know how many shooters were with the woman. We have the diamond, and that's all that matters. Bear will survive. We safely got out of the building. Kim skidded up to the curve just in time. "I got the door." Redd opened it and aimed his weapon towards the museum so that we wouldn't get flanked. "Slowly." Smoke said while handling the big man. "Right," I responded. I wasn't thinking about moving slow. We need to leave immediately. "C'mon. Hurry the fuck up for the cops show." Kim yelled. She was right and I shoved Bear big ass in the car. "Ah," Bear groaned and grabbed his shoulder. You'll live. Bear groans made me feel like a huge wild animal was dying. I'm grateful his legs were able to function. If he had been hit below the waist. I'm not sure we could've carried him and got out alive. We got Bear inside the car. Redd was the last to get in. The sound of the tires peeling out sounded good.

Chapter 54

FIVE MINUTES BEFORE

Abel hopped inside the vent, followed by Snake. BAM positioned on the roof to watch for any other activity. Abel's adrenaline began to rush through his body as he crawled through the ventilation system. He thought about having to kill the cleaners to get the diamond. He planned for a few scenarios. He looked at Snake, and he was close behind. Everything was going according to plan. He radioed Gina from the vent. "Gina, my love. What is your position?" "I'm walking the halls." She said. "The guards in the front are done. They're taking a long nap. I'm on my way to the diamond room. This is easier than I thought it would be. I radioed Ali. He has control over the cameras. He's monitoring everything. You're clear to move. I'll meet you at the checkpoint, my love. Abel grinned. "I'll meet you there. Move with caution. There could be more guards that we're not aware of. You know what to do in any situation." "I do, my love." Abel radioed Ali. "I need the location of the diamond? Did they remove it from the case?" Ali didn't notice the three mask men following Gina. He was busy gawking at her body, aroused by her hourglass figure. The first girl he fell in love with he raped and killed. It turned him into a psycho genius. "Good news, the vent leads directly to the diamond room. It's out of the case and the cleaning process has begun. I'm clocking it. You have eight minutes. And by the way, the case is unbreakable." "Copy that," Abel said. "Are there any more guards?" "I'm monitoring Gina. So far, so... hold on a minute. "He said hesitantly. "We have a problem. There seem to be two masked men with guns following her. Shit, another one just came into view. Make that three masked men." "Someone followed her into the museum?" Abel asked skeptically. "If my intelligence serves me correctly." He said. "Yes and no. There was no way they followed her into the museum. Unless someone told them about our plan, I assume they're after the diamond. Maybe The Planner sent a second team? Your guess is good as mine, sir." "Ok, keep me updated." Abel turned to Snake. "We have to hurry. Someone's trying to intercept the diamond." He hustled through the vent and came to the room with the diamond. He overheard a male voice speaking to Gina. He slowly unbolted the vent. The last screw fell and made a soft ting against the metal. He held up a closed fist signaling for Snake to pause. He was trying not to alert the men of their presence. After a moment of silence, Abel cautiously pushed the vent open without making a sound. He peeped his head out just enough to see a huge man holding Gina captive. He immediately stuck his arm out of the vent. He aimed with precision at the giant's shoulder away from Gina. It was too risky to aim for a headshot. He pulled the trigger and saw Gina run out of the room. Target down, one of them was hurt. He quickly looked in the room. A man wearing a black mask returned fire. He retreated before his head exploded. "What the fuck!" He stuck his arm out and fired. He wanted to hit somebody. He thought they all could die. He unloaded a full clip. They couldn't take his diamond. His plans for power would be destroyed. "Dammit." Snake was anxious to do some damage but was trapped behind Abel. It wasn't safe to drop. Bullets were nearly piercing through the metal vent. Abel's blood began to simmer. They were trying to take his diamond. The Planner had sent another team. He was facing a major problem. He fired his gun until he heard it click. He got back in cover while reloading his last clip. "They're not getting my diamond!" He roared before sticking his body halfway out the vent. He was caught by surprise. There was nobody to aim at in the room. The cleaners were still alive and thought about killing them. The mask men were gone with his diamond. "Fuck!" Ali radioed Abel. "I have a name for one of the masked men that was in the room with Gina. After running a face scan from the footage, I caught on video. His name is Simon Jones. He went to your high school, the same year you attended."

Chapter 55
WOUNDED BEAR -KANE-

I sat next to Bear in the backseat. I told Kim to drive. She looked back and saw blood, and it startled her. Kim spoke, "Hospital?" We have to think rationally. If we take him straight to the hospital, they will ask questions. He's shot, and we're dressed in black. The cops would be called. I looked at Bear's wound and tried to figure out if the bullet traveled through. Kim kept driving while waiting for instructions. This is a serious situation. Two dead guards, a mystery woman, and her team. They would be looking for us because of the diamond. Do I really want to risk all of us going to prison? I told Kim to drive to the apartment after I investigated the wound. He's a big guy. I think he'll be alright. Kim will have to treat the injury when we're safe. I remember scraping my knee after running over a player on the football field. My knee collided with his helmet and tore off some skin. Kim walked with me to the nurse's office after practice. Nobody was in at the time, so Kim went through the office supplies like she owned the place. I asked her what she was doing, and she said, just relax. She found what she was looking for and went to work on my wound. We made it to the apartment safely. Kim went ahead to unlock the door. Bear regained some strength and didn't need our help to walk. He got out of the car while holding his shoulder. He groaned a few times, but overall, he was good. Bear is the only person I've ever seen up close larger than Big Bruce. Bear could probably survive under more severe conditions. Kim was ready to work some magic on his shoulder. She told him to sit in the dining room chair. The bleeding had slowed down. I told him to keep pressure on the wound. I knew that from watching too many action movies. Smoke and Redd sat in the living room. They began talking about what went wrong at the museum. Kim had got a first aid kit from the bathroom. She cut his shirt off where the wound was located. It didn't look that bad. She told Bear to close his eyes. She began stitching the injury. I was surprised when she revealed a lighter. What? Burning the wound will keep it from getting infected. That was the first time I heard Bear cry. Finally, she rubbed ointment over the surface and wrapped a bandage around his arm. The bullet went through at an angle. It won't take that long to heal. He's good. Suddenly, my phone began to ring.

Chapter 56

DIAMOND INVESTIGATION
-JORDAN-

I looked at the clock. "Two thirty." I'm tired to death and my phone is ringing. I rolled over and reached for it on the nightstand. I checked the caller I.D. to see who was calling. "Rick, what is it? It's two thirty in the morning. This better be good if you're bothering me this late?" Rick sounded like he was wide awake from drinking coffee all night. "Jordan, I need you to come to the museum. There's been a robbery." "Robbery?" I wanted to make sure I heard him correctly. "At the museum?" "Do you remember our first case together?" "The diamond we had to watch for the museum when the Africans were threatening to steal it?" "Yes, exactly." He assured me. "Someone figured out how to steal it. I got the call and I'm on my way there now. The heist wasn't the only thing that went down. Two security guards were murdered." "Someone was actually able to steal the diamond and murdered two security guards? Is that what you're implying?" I got out of bed and slid on my pants. "Yes," He assured. "That's what I said." "Ok, give me thirty minutes. I'm on the way." I hung up the phone with Rick. I walked into the bathroom and began brushing my teeth. I ran a hot rag over my face. That's one way to overcome feeling the way I felt. Late night investigations are not meant for me. I rather stay home and sleep. Usually, the suspect escapes before you get out of bed. Then your phone rings. I finished getting ready and drove to the museum. I parked the car and called Rick. "I'm here." "Jordan," Rick answered. "I'm inside the museum. Where are you exactly?" "I just parked the car." "Let's meet in front of the building." He said. "I want to let you know what I think before you head inside." "I'm on the way." I ended the call and put the phone in my pocket. I even left my gun in the glove compartment. No action tonight. That's why I hate night jobs. The cops are the first to get the call. We're next in line, depending on the situation. The suspect could make a clean getaway by the time we arrive on the scene. I double checked for my badge. If you had that type of power, you wouldn't leave home without it either. There are fewer police officers on the scene than I had thought. I spotted two ambulances parked outside. More than likely here for the security guards. I stopped two EMT workers carrying one of the victims on a gurney. I flashed my badge. "Hold on a second. I need to check this guy out." I told them. I wanted to see how he died. The cause of death can sometimes be useful. "It's bad," One spoke up. "Sure, you have the stomach for it?" "Absolutely," I replied. "If his head is still attached, I'll be alright." They lowered the gurney to the ground. I signed to expose the upper half of the body. "Holy crap." I was startled by the exceptional look on the victim's face. Face stiffness and lockjaw. He looked like he was screaming and I wouldn't doubt he saw a ghost. I'm looking at a character from a horror film. I've never witnessed a more horrific facial expression. "What was the cause of death?" "He was poisoned." Poisoned? That's interesting. "Do you know how?" I stood and signed for them to cover the body. I saw what I had to see. Any longer and I'll have to hire a psychologist. "It's hard to comprehend the cause of death." He said. "I examined the body with a ultraviolet light. I discovered poison on his lips that has the same strength as snake venom. He died immediately. He could've drunk something harmful or kissed by the poisonous chick in the Bat movie." "That broad is hot." The other commented. "She can poison me." "What if she wanted to give you head, first?" His partner asked. The funny guy was lost for words. "Exactly," His partner sounded serious. "Your fucking dick will rot off." I've heard enough. "Thank you." I walked to the front of the museum. A kiss, damn. That means a woman was involved, or he drunk something deadly. I approached Rick at the front door. "What's going on?" I asked before entering the building. "You get a look at the guard?" "Yes, poison." Rick said. "The look on his face gave me the chills. It's the same for the other guard." He paused. "What I wanted to tell you is I think our dread head friends committed this crime."

Chapter 57
THE CONSULT -KANE-

The name on the caller I.D. surprised me. "Abel." My brother had never called this late. He was probably thinking about our parents. I don't have time to play big bro. Ask me about the past two years, if anything. I walked into the bedroom to speak in private. I answered the phone. "Bro, what are you doing up this late?" I tried to sound concerned. "Nothing," He sounded tired. "Just got back in the house." "Really, where are you coming from?" "I went to a bar and grill with a friend." "You, out?" Should I be concerned? My brother never went out to go anywhere. He doesn't like drinking or partying. He could be trying something new. "Needed a break from studying? I gotcha." "I don't study all the time." He assured me. "I'm human. I get out occasionally with my girlfriend." "Wha... you, a girlfriend? That's amazing. I'll have to meet her one day. We can go on a double date." I wanted to get off the phone. Rushing him off the line could be a bad idea. He needed someone to talk to, and I rather talk than push him further out of my life. We never had a deep conversation. If I pushed him away, that would be pushing the last family member I have left out the door. Abel is blood, and the reality of our father's death probably just hit. Liquor will do that to you. "Perhaps." He didn't sound interested. "I have a question." I held my hand over the phone and peeped out the door. There was a lot of commotion coming from the living room. I saw Smoke pretending to shoot a gun while he was explaining to Redd what happened in the diamond room. Kim and Bear were also listening to his story. I shut the door. "Yeah, what is it?" For a moment, I felt concerned, even after everything he had done. It's a feeling I cannot explain. He's still my brother. "Were you in Atlanta around two in the morning?" He asked. "I thought I saw you when we passed by the museum." The question startled me. I should have answered it faster, but my mouth was stuck in an open position. I needed to lie. It shouldn't have been difficult to answer. There is a possibility he saw us driving from the museum. So, what if he did see us? I'm old enough to party with some friends. I played it cool. "Nah, that wasn't me." I wanted him to trust me. "Kim and I ordered a movie on demand. I don't need to be out anywhere this late. I have to look for a job. All work, no play." "Are you sure that wasn't you?" He pressed.

"Positive, Kim would've killed me. She's serious about me finding a job." I flipped the switch. "Have you been to see mom?" I was confused and surprised at the same time. I was speaking with a dial tone. He hung up the phone before I could finish? I thought about calling back. I wanted to get off the phone, so I wasn't mad. Mentioning our mother probably upset him. That's not an excuse for not visiting her. He's been grieving and I understand how he felt. I was about to leave the room and the phone rang a second time. Unknown caller. "Who's this?" "You know who this is and I know you have the diamond. You did a wonderful job. I watched the news. Meet me at the new restaurant on 17th street at 3 o'clock sharp." The Planner, before I could respond. He ended the call.

Chapter 58
RESTAURANT LOVE-

I will finally meet The Planner today at the new restaurant on 17th street. I stayed up all night, thinking about being five million dollars richer. That's now a possibility. If he turns his back on me and I don't get the money. What then? I just sat there staring into space, wondering if I would get paid. That wouldn't be a good situation for any of us. And if that happens, what will I do? I don't know anybody else who would buy the diamond. The Planner needs to make good on this deal, or there will be trouble. I'll need backup, so I called Smoke. I can depend on him with something of this magnitude. This will be my first time seeing The Planner. I couldn't visualize his face without hearing his real voice. He could be anybody. I'll be vulnerable until he contacts me at three. The only thing I can do is sit at one of the tables outside of the restaurant. It gives me a better vantage point while not worrying about exposing myself to danger. He wouldn't try to kill me in public if he wants the diamond, but I rather be safe. My phone rang, vibrating the living room table. I reached for it, Smoke. "I'm in front when you're ready." He sounded cool. "A'ight, I'll be down in a few seconds." At the time, I meant it. Kim came out before I could open the door. She had just got out of the shower. She probably heard me getting ready over the water. She stood in front of me, soaking wet and naked. I gave her my attention. All I could think was damn, look at her. She could wake the dead with her body. "Where do you think you're going?" She was seductive when asking. Man, what am I supposed to do with her standing in front of me like that with water glistening all over her body? Her breasts are perfectly round with a body shaped like a coke bottle. Dammit. Why now? She's making it tough to leave. Why am I contemplating? I need to get myself together and focus. Even though I highly considered staying. I reluctantly passed. "I have to meet The Planner. Smoke is waiting out front. He's giving me a ride and watching my back. I told you about our meeting at the restaurant. Why are you trying to play me like this? Standing here seducing me by being wet and naked." She smiled. "Well, I guess I'll have to work by myself?" I took a deep breath. "Can you wait until I come back? You can go shopping to keep your mind off me being gone." I had stashed the forty thousand I took from the robbery in a shoebox. I grabbed two stacks and tossed her the money. A smile instantly spread across her face. I don't mind spending money on my woman even though she had her own. She took care of me when I got out of jail. Why wouldn't I treat her the same? "We'll pick this conversation up when I return. I want you to get something nice to wear for tonight. And buy me some new J's with a matching snapback. I wanna be fresh when I'm hitting that." "I want some when you get back home and no excuses." She looked at me a certain way when she said it. "You're uh freak." And I wasn't being sarcastic. "You made me this way." She countered. "I think we made each other this way." I paused before I said. "I'll see you later." I watched her ass while she walked away. Control yourself. My father told me never to get caught in a woman's spell when there is work to be done. It could be your downfall. Work first, play second. I grabbed the diamond from a box I hid it in after the museum heist. I unwrapped the sock it was inside and held it up to the closet light. I spun it around slowly, amazed at what I had in my possession. I smiled. "Five mill," I muttered. After a brief moment of being mesmerized, I tucked the diamond in my pouch and strapped it around my shoulder. Kim had returned to the shower. I heard her singing over the water. I lifted the end of the mattress, where I hid the Beretta. I tucked it in my waistband and fixed my shirt over it. I checked the mirror to make sure it was secure. Cool, I'm ready to roll. I grabbed my cell phone off the living room table and locked the door after I left the apartment. I saw my friend. "Smoke." I approached the car. "What's good?" Smoke unlocked the door. "Shit, coolin'. I was beginning to think you didn't want the money?" He said sarcastically. "I've been waiting damn near an hour." I shut the door and gave him some dap. I adjusted the seat because the gun was poking me in the side. "Please, you haven't been waiting that long. You just called." I reminded him. "You would've waited anyway. You know we have to get this money. Did you bring your strap?" "You know it." "Let's ride. Hit the new restaurant on 17th street." I told him. "We're supposed to meet him there at three. It's two thirty, so we have some time. We need to get a table outside of the building. It'll be safer while we wait for his call." "Good because I'm hungry. I've thought about trying their food. This girl I know told me they have some slamming hamburgers." He grabbed his stomach and squeezed. He started the car and drove out of the neighborhood. We were listening to King Coopa J's new song. Smoke has a top of the line stereo system. The bass was hitting hard. I bobbed my head to the beat. Damn, it was motivating me to get money. After a moment of driving, Smoke reached in the ashtray. What? Smoke, smoked? I didn't notice the smell before. He came to a red light and lit the blunt. He bobbed his head, listening to the music. He turned on the air ventilation so the smell wouldn't stay trapped inside the car. He held the blunt up, offering me to hit the weed. "You want to hit it? It's that Kush." Kush? What the hell is Kush? There are different names for weed? The aroma was the same smell as the weed I smoked with Kim. Were we smoking Kush? "Nah man, I'm cool. I appreciate it, though." He shrugged and hit it again before putting it out in the ashtray. I didn't want to come off lame, but I have to stay focus. Who knows what I'll do while on drugs in public. My reactions slowed down when I smoked. Smoke's eyes were low and red. It didn't take long for him to get high. I might be high from second hand smoke. "That's the spot over there." I pointed to a brick building on the corner. The restaurant had an island effect. We drove into a nice size parking lot. The place was definitely doing some good business. The lot was almost full. Five minutes had passed before we found a space to park the car. I made sure the gun was loaded before getting out of the vehicle. Smoke opened the glove compartment and grabbed his pistol. He tucked the weapon under his shirt. I checked everything I had on me, my cell phone, money for food, strap, and the diamond. I'm good to go. I was paranoid while walking through the parking lot. This is the first time I carried a weapon in a public place with this amount of people. Not to mention a stolen diamond I knew could send me to the feds. The pressure was on, but I kept my composure. Smoke got the door, and we stepped inside the restaurant. We approached the host desk at the front. She was dressed in island clothes that matched the scenery. "Welcome to the Bahamas." She greeted us with a smile. "Yeah, well-come-to-the-BA-Hamas." Smoke was flirting with the hostess. She smiled at him. She was cute as hell. She had long dark brown hair, hazel eyes, caramel skin, and a very nice body. She looked Bahamian. If I wasn't with Kim, she could get it. "Can we get a table outside?" "Can I get your number?" Smoke asked, coolly leaning on the desk. She kept smiling while looking through a book on the desk. I glanced over her counter. She was checking the availability of the tables. "I'm sorry, I'm not allowed to give my number out while on the clock." Her finger scanned the lines searching for an open spot. "What time you get off the clock? I'll swing back through... for you." He offered. I didn't know Smoke had so much game. He had this woman blushing. I could tell she was interested. She signed for us to follow her. Smoke whispered to me on the way to our table. "She's going to be my woman." She turned her head around and smiled. I'm sure she heard Smoke because he wasn't quiet about it. It could've been a high moment. That's my dawg, though. She showed us our table. The outside view was nice from where we were seated. She gave us menus. Before she left the table, she looked at Smoke seductively and said. "Four."

Chapter 59

ONE HIT WONDER-

We ordered some food. I checked the time on my phone. "Five more minutes." I muttered. The Planner will call soon with the details. I grabbed my pouch and felt the diamond from the outside. I've done a lot for this moment. The first thing I'll do is get my mother out of the hospital. A vacation would be nice until things cooled down. The waiter returned with our food. She gently set the plates on the table. I looked at the hamburger I had ordered. I wasn't hungry anymore. I'm more anxious to get the deal done. Smoke didn't feel the same about his food. The thought of having five million dollars clouded my mind. "Three minutes." I took a bite of my burger and couldn't taste anything. I was in the zone. "One minute." My phone rested on the table next to my plate. The Planner will call any minute. Smoke only focused on his burger. Suddenly, my phone rang. The Planner. I answered.

Smoke concentrated on me. His mouth was full of food and his eyes were wide. "The Planner?" I barely understood with all the food in his mouth. I held up a finger for him to give me a moment of silence. "Are you at the restaurant?" A broken radio voice spoke. The Planner is on the line. I glanced around the restaurant nonchalantly, hoping to spot someone on their cell phone. I figured he had to be somewhere close. The Planner wouldn't be foolish enough to bring the money here with this many people inside. The transaction will have to get done in a different location. If I'm to get paid, it wouldn't be here, and not being able to plan accordingly made me feel uneasy. "Yeah, I'm here." I said nonchalantly. "Where are you?" "That's none of your concern," He told me. "Just pay attention to the instructions I'm about to give you. Do you understand?" "Yeah, whatever." I answered with a little sarcasm. "I'm listening." "A black BMW is waiting in the front parking lot. Get in the back passenger seat." I felt hesitant about the situation. I'll be vulnerable as hell, but I've come too far to stop. I have to think fast without knowing my next location. Now I'm concerned. I hung up the phone. "Smoke," I said seriously. "I need you to follow a black BMW. It's waiting for me in front." He had a confused look on his face. "You understand?" "Black BMW, why?" He said, raising his eyebrows. "I'm sure The Planner is taking me to a discreet location. Listen, I don't have that much time. Just do as I say. Leave now so you can be ready. I'll call you and put the call on speaker. Mute your phone to avoid any sounds. You will know if I get in any trouble." I assured him. After he left, I called his phone. He was in the car when he answered. I heard the vehicle start. I locked the phone, so I wouldn't accidentally end the call. I have to be on point to get through this safely. I tossed a hundred-dollar bill on the center of the table. That covered our bill plus a seventy-dollar tip. I felt like being generous. Hopefully, that luck will swing back around. I would have enjoyed the meal on any other day, but not today. I walked out of the restaurant. I spotted the black BMW. A man dressed in a suit stood beside the vehicle. The Planner? He wouldn't make it that easy. I signaled to him and he nodded. I walked over while praying this wouldn't be my last ride.

Chapter 60
BOSS MOVE-

I'm the only person in the vehicle besides the driver. He drove off. Smoke was in position. We rode in silence for the first mile. I paid close attention to where he was driving. He didn't say a word the entire time. He focused on the road. I saw his eyes look at me through the rearview. He wasn't secretive about it. He wanted to let me know he was watching. He probably thinks I'm paranoid. I kept my cool. I have a feeling this guy is a killer for hire. "Where are we going?" Enough with the silent treatment. "Are we meeting The Planner?" "Almost there." He said in a deep harsh voice. "Where are you taking me?" "Be patient, almost there." I'm not trying to hear we're almost there. Something is wrong about this guy. My instincts told me to watch out. I have to concentrate on not losing my composure. Every second that passed, I became more frustrated. The car was moving at the speed limit. Smoke was still in the clear. Hopefully, he's keeping a safe distance. We finally arrived at a warehouse. The building was old and abandoned. He turned around and looked me in the eyes. "You brought the diamond?" "You brought my money?" I saw a grin on his face. His eyes trailed off to the side. Something caught his attention. He got out of the car. I looked back and Smoke saw behind the vehicle. Fuck. The driver probably thinks we're trying to set him up. This situation just got ugly. I saw the driver remove a pistol from the inside of his coat. Shit. I tried to unlock the door to get out. Child safety locks. Damn. I ducked in the seat to cover from gunfire. I pulled out my Beretta and took that bitch off safety. Planner or not, this guy is about to get the business. He ran to the front of the car. Shit. I couldn't get a clear shot. I spotted Smoke in cover. He was alive. I saw bullet holes in his windshield. He quickly maneuvered behind the driver's side door. That was a good move because the gunman was firing inside the car. I heard the front window shatter. I swiftly shielded myself behind the driver seat. This guy was definitely trying to kill me. I should've never trusted The Planner. I swayed my pistol from side to side, aiming through the front window, trying to catch the diver being careless. My sides were unguarded, and if he shoots through the back windshield, I'm done. At least the windows are a dark tint. I couldn't see through them from the outside. That somewhat works to my advantage. For now,

Smoke is my only protection. I heard him call out my name. I did the same, assuring him that I was still breathing. This is my second shootout, two days' worth of life-threatening drama. I checked the ignition. The driver left me a trump card. The keys. I instantly came up with a plan. "Smoke," I shouted. "Where is he?" I needed to know where the gunman was before I proceed. One wrong move and I'm dead. I waited for an answer. I heard more gunshots. This time the shots were coming from a distance. Smoke held him off by returning fire. I heard Smoke call out. "Right side." Shit, he maneuvered to the passenger side. He knows we have the edge. I focused my attention on that side of the vehicle. The windows were still intact, but the side mirrors were damaged. I'm going for it. I rather get shot trying to escape than sitting here like prey. I crawled between the seats to the front. I was good and swiftly started the car. The driver fired into the vehicle after hearing the engine rev. I sped off before he got a clear shot. I drifted the car 180 degrees. The transition was smooth, and I successfully stopped by Smoke's car. I searched for the driver through the rearview mirror and found him in the open without any type of cover. He fired at the vehicle while scrambling around like a wild man. He acted as if he caught a bullet. I'm not about to leave the car, so I had to think of something quick. The driver was acting frantic while firing his weapon. Fuck it, I put the BMW in reverse and floored the gas pedal. I kept my eyes on the driver through the back window. I aimed the rear end of the car at the gunman, and he stood there, unaware of my plan. He realized what was unfolding and tried to evade impact. The tail end smacked him in midair as he tried to dive away. The collision violently jerked his body in the opposite direction. He recklessly came to a rolling stop. I turned my attention to Smoke. "You good?" I rolled down the window, so I was clear. He was standing behind his car door. He gave me a thumbs up. I nodded at the sign. He walked over to the vehicle while holding the pistol in his right hand. I don't blame him. I sighed, relieved I didn't die in the end. I relaxed in the seat and closed my eyes to concentrate. Who the hell was that guy? The Planner wanted me dead. What if I didn't bring the diamond? Then what? Does he think I'm that stupid? He wouldn't take a chance without confirming. I felt a tap on the shoulder. I was caught by surprise, and I aimed the gun at the person's head. "Damn, my fault. I fucking forgot you walked over." I lowered the gun. My mind was exhausted, and my next move needs to be great. "It's alright." Smoke sounded relieved. "At least you didn't blow my head off. C'mon, let's leave before more guys like him show up." "No problem, but I want to see if he's dead. I need to find out something if he's still alive." I got out of the car. It wasn't the same vehicle. Bullet holes covered the surface front to back. The front windshield was shattered, and the rear end has a huge dent. Total wreck. I'm grateful to still be on planet earth. Smoke and I approached the gunman. He was barely alive, and that's good enough for me. His mouth filled with blood. His body twitched every five seconds, fighting death. His clothes were dusty and torn. The collision was devastating. His gun was amazingly still in his grip. I would've been dead if he had enough strength to move. He wasn't in any condition to kill anybody, he failed. Suddenly, he swiftly placed the gun to his head. He would rather kill himself than have one of us take his life. I thought about putting a bullet between his eyes. My finger was still on the trigger. I never imagined catching a body. Ask me that after seeing Big Bruce for the first time. That's not the type of guy you don't want to box on your best day. "Are you The Planner?" I asked sternly. The gunman had a crazy look on his face. He smiled like he wanted to die. He started coughing up blood. He kept the gun pressed to the temple of his head. I glanced at Smoke, and he shrugged. My attention moved back to the gunman. "Where is The Planner?" I became slightly frustrated. He never answered and kept smiling at me like a stupid person. "Do it." Right then, the gun exploded. His brains flew out the side of his head onto the pavement. Shit like this only happened in movies. The driver took his own life. The old Kane would've been shocked. After what I've been through. I understand what survival means. If you want the short version... exist.

Chapter 61
SHOPPER'S LIST-

Kim turned off the car in the mall parking lot. She grabbed her purse from the passenger seat and unplugged her cell phone from the charger. She made a list of things she wanted to purchase. One of the items was a new varsity jacket and hat for Kane. She saw the set two weeks ago when he was on a steady job hunt. The jacket and matching hat momentarily captured his attention. She noticed how bad he felt after seeing the three-hundred-dollar price tag. He looked unhappy. She couldn't imagine how he felt and remembered saying to herself. When I get the money, that's the first thing I'll buy for my man. He probabl y feels saddened by not having the money. I'll come back in a week when I get paid. Fortunately, things turned out differently. She locked the doors to her Lexus. She planned to leave the clothes in the open, so he could see them when he came home. She thought about Kane before herself. That's how much she loves him. He makes her feel better than anyone. If loving him means robbing a bank or stealing a diamond. It's done. Her love for him is strong. She hurried through the front entrance of the mall. She failed to notice two men following her every step. The men followed her from the apartment. She didn't prepare for conflict. Her mind was on shopping for her boyfriend, the love of her life. She walked inside the store that had the matching set on display. The store assistant met her at the door. The young lady smiled graciously and asked if she needed help finding anything. She looked about sixteen years old with a petite body. She knew why they hired them young and cute with a bright attitude. Eighty percent of the time, they could persuade the shopper to buy. Kim smiled lively at the girl, remembering the time when she was in the same position. "Yes, I do. I'm looking for the varsity jacket and hat that was on display here about two weeks ago." "Oh, I remember." She said kindly. "I think we might have one set in the back. Give me a second to check, please." She hurried off and returned with the varsity gear. It was perfect. "Great," Kim said brightly. I'll take it." She paid and tipped the girl a ten. She spent the next two hours shopping after leaving the store. She made it to the car while carrying four bags, two in each hand. She sat them down and rummaged through her purse for the keys. Suddenly, her mouth was forcefully covered. She wasn't able to fight and slowly felt herself fading away. The struggle finally ended. Her vision was swallowed by darkness.

THE END

My Brother's Keeper

BOOK II

Chapter 1
HELP WANTED -KANE-

On the ride back to the apartment. I was trying to conceive what just happened at the warehouse. The Planner sent a trained killer. Smoke and I didn't speak. He probably thought about his share of the money. At this point, we could only imagine that much cash. Everything we had planned was now ruined. I have a diamond worth millions and don't know who else to sell it to. I don't have another buyer. I thought about the bank robbery and the heist. The two crimes I committed after being framed for murder. Trouble seems to follow me around now. I thought for certain things would get better after I sold the rock to The Planner. That's far from happening now. I should have expected a guy like that would try to kill me. The only option I have is to wait for him to call. The thought of putting myself in danger a second time is a shame. I'm asking to die. I adjusted the seat to a more relaxing position and took a deep breath. I don't have a million questions like some people. I only need the answer to one. If somebody can answer me out there in a world people take for granted. I would greatly appreciate it. I didn't expect my life to turn out this way, I was good. I had the best family anyone could ever ask for. Things changed and everything suddenly went south. Why? That's the only question I need someone to answer. Why? The question behind every remark. A simple word that seems to be more of a comeback question. I wonder what my friends would want to know? Smoke would ask about his grandmother. Why did she have to die at sixty-five? Redd, why didn't he have a stronger leg? People recover from leg injuries, but he didn't. Bear would want to know why he had to be the one with a sleeping disorder. He could have been an amazing football player. Kim would ask about not receiving a track scholarship. She was one of the top runners in the state at the time. Many things in life are left unexplained. You just have to take the road that was chosen for you without question. I took the diamond out of my pouch and gave it a mean stare. I turned it side to side. I came close to death two times for this fucking rock. The value of this thing is life-threatening. What the hell was I thinking of when I decided to steal it in the first place? I saw Smoke glance at it. "What do you think we should do?" I broke the silence without looking at him. My attention was on the death rock. "About what?" He asked in a calm voice. "Everything," I whispered. "Starting with this. What do you suggest we do with this damn thing? This... this shit is getting crazy. I mean... what I'm trying to say is... I never pictured us as criminals. Man... we have been best friends since high school. We're supposed to be living it up right now. Running, balling, football, whatever." I felt my emotions taking over. "We were good at everything. The best and nobody could touch us. How can something so good turn out this damn bad?" I felt my blood simmering. Smoke was silent. Maybe he was remembering those moments in high school when we blew out our competition. Somebody is about to get smoked. Two high school state titles in track. That's what the phrase meant. Man... those were the days. Look at the person I've become since then. My father would disown me for what I've done. And he's the one who told me to take care of my mother by any means necessary. The car pulled into the apartments. I was ready to get out when Smoke spoke up. "Kane, we do what we have to do. You're smarter than you think. I trusted you with the bank and the museum heist. Call me insane, but I didn't do it because you're my friend. I did it because I believe in you." He smiled. I closed my fist and gave my best friend some dap. I needed that. I went into the apartment feeling better. Kim wasn't home. I was exhausted from everything that happened today. I walked directly to the bedroom and crashed on the bed. Now I know how tired you can get from a gun battle.

Chapter 2
WAKE UP CALL

"How do I catch the ball?" I asked. "It's bigger than me." My father walked over and showed me how to spread my fingers. He was teaching me how to catch a football. "Keep your finger's apart son and when the ball comes in your direction. Wrap your hands around it, ok?" I held my hands out with my fingers spread just like he told me. "But... I'm scared." He walked about ten yards away from me. I followed close behind and made it two yards before he told me to stop. He said I'm supposed to be a few feet away. I had to stay put and catch an enormous ball. "There's no reason to be scared, son. The ball won't hurt you." I held my hands out while still trying to follow my father. The helmet felt too big for my head. My skull felt heavier than before. I couldn't see straight with it covering my eyes. I wanted to take it off. I felt a sudden sting in my stomach. "Ouch!" He had thrown the ball and it hit me in the center of my chest. I wasn't ready for it and I started to cry. I left the ball on the ground and walked in his direction. When I made it to him, the air in my three-year-old chest slowly returned. He ran in the opposite direction towards the ball. The oversized helmet caused me to walk off-balance. My hands were in a catch position as I followed behind him. The blow to my chest brought tears to my eyes. I didn't like the football game we were playing. I wanted to stop. I felt the ball hit my hands. It stung a little, but not like the first time. I continued forward with my hands out and tripped face forward over the ball. "Ouch." My hands hit the ground. The helmet felt like a block of stone and I collapsed on the ground. Grass and dirt got in my mouth. It was hard to get up. I thought my father was walking over to pick me up. Instead, he grabbed the football and ran in the opposite direction. Somewhere, the distinct sound of my brother laughing could be heard. His voice was clear and not inspiring. I got up from the ground and noticed my father standing in the distance. For some reason, my hands were out with my fingers spread apart. I walked towards him. "I hate foo..." I felt a sting in my hands. The world around me became silent. The sound of my brother laughing, couldn't be heard anymore. I was no longer crying as I continued walking towards my father, ready to end my football career in three catch attempts. I opened my eyes to see if he was in front of me. Surprisingly, I saw my hands wrapped around the football. I caught it! I approached my father and spiked the ball on the ground. He picked me up and tossed me into the air while cheering. He sounded proud of me. "You caught the ball son! That's my boy." Maybe that was all the inspiration I needed. I caught the football for the first time in my life at the age of three. What a birthday. A loud sound woke me from my dream. I remembered that day vividly. I didn't drop a football again until my sophomore year of high school. Only because I collided with another receiver on the team while going after the ball simultaneously. His fault if you want to know the truth. My side of the field, my route. That was my final season before I got arrested for murder. I looked at the clock, 3:45 am. The alarm sounded. I set the timer when I was searching for a job and forgot to turn it off. I rolled over to get some more rest. Something didn't feel quite right. I checked the time again to assure there was no confusion, 3:46 am. I set up. Strange, I didn't notice this before, Kim was not in the bed.

Chapter 3
MISSING PERSON

My curiosity level rose every second. "Where's Kim?" I felt like a bag of bones. My body, put up a fight as I got out of bed. I had to command my legs to operate. They felt paralyzed. I walked off the numb feeling heading into the living room. I needed some water immediately. My mouth was dry as the Arizona desert. My mind went back to Kim. Perhaps she went out with a friend? That suggestion spent a short amount of time in my mind. No way, she's not the stay out type. Work? Another suggestion that wasn't the right answer. Damn, where could she have gone? I was beginning to seriously worry about her whereabouts. I finished the glass of water. It helped a little. At least my cottonmouth was gone. This had to be how my father felt about my mother. Welcome to stress. There's a possibility she stayed out cheating with another guy. I smiled at that. Perfect time to do it when I gained forty grand in cash and a diamond worth millions. Ok, I shouldn't think about her that way. That was stupid. Damn, I'm getting desperate. I left the kitchen and sat in complete darkness in the living room. If I didn't know any better, I resembled an angry husband, waiting in the middle of the night for his cheating wife to come home. Is this how married people act? Apparently so. My eyes were wide, anticipating her to walk through the door at any moment. What other alternative do I have? Maybe, I should have stayed home. The Planner tried to kill me and now Kim is suddenly missing. I don't know what to think or how to feel. "Shit," I whispered. I thought back to when I switched my phone on vibrate after Smoke and I left the restaurant. How did I forget something like that? What if she tried to call my phone? I hurried to the bedroom. I picked up my pants and grabbed my phone from the left pocket. No, it was dead. I drained the battery. Charger. Where is it? I never misplace it. Now it's gone. Shit. Where did I put that damn thing? I search the entire bedroom with sonic boom speed. I couldn't find it anywhere. Ok, calm down. The living room? I frantically checked the entire area. I felt my heart rate speed up to 200 mph. My adrenaline took over. This could be important. What if something serious happened? I stopped searching to gather my thoughts. I could have a heart attack at the speed I was moving. Think, where was the last place you charged your phone? I didn't, Kim used it. She needs a new one so she borrowed mine. Bedroom, living room, kitchen? She used it in the kitchen. I hurried to the kitchen. Bingo. Right there in front of my face. My charger was plugged into the wall. I connected it to my phone and waited a minute before it gained some power. I had seven missed calls. None were from Kim. What, why? I called her phone five times. Each call ended in her voicemail. I sat on the sofa perplexed. I accidentally turned on the TV by sitting on the remote control. The news turned on. "Oh, my God." Kim's car had been abandoned at the mall. The news headline read, Possible Missing Person.

ABOUT
THE AUTHOR

New York Times & International Best Selling Author
Billie Dureyea Shell was born in Compton California and now
lives in Ladera Heights with his wife and
kids who he loves to spend time with.
He is the Owner of several properties in the Los Angeles area
and gives back to his community by providing low income
housing to those who need it.
He stated "It doesn't matter where you at or where you from
it's what you do with your time. There's nothing you can't do
if you put your mind to it".